ONE NIGHT WITH THE CEO

CEO SERIES

EMILY HAYES

GENEVIEVE

Genevieve Mitchell trudged out of the office. She made an effort to smile at her employees and congratulate them on their good work. This wasn't their fault. They had all performed excellently, as usual. No, this was Genevieve's blunder. She had really hoped that they would be able to work out a deal with this potential new client, but in the end, it hadn't worked out.

He would have been a huge asset to Wisdom Investments, and thus was entitled to some concessions in order to draw him in. However, he was simply asking for too much. If Genevieve had agreed to his terms, it would have taken five years for them to start making real profit from his portfolio, and who's to say he wouldn't have moved to another company by then?

As much as she regretted not being able to land the deal, Genevieve hadn't worked her way up to CEO of her father's company by taking stupid risks. Calculated risks, yes, but this one would have been foolish.

Her phone started ringing. Genevieve grimaced, knowing who it would be. Her father knew about the meeting and would be eager to hear how it went. Genevieve let the call go to voice mail. She would deal with her father's disappointment later.

He would encourage her, to be sure, but that wouldn't take away from the invisible but real pressure he put on Genevieve to excel in her field.

That pressure had made her into a better CEO, and she didn't resent him for it, but it did make dealing with her family difficult at times.

Genevieve was halfway home when she decided that she didn't want to go home to her sad, empty apartment and wallow in her own failure.

She hadn't gotten laid in a while, as busy as she had been trying to work this deal. It was a perfect night to resolve that.

She headed to a local bar, Lix Club- an exclusive women's only club which was one of her favorites for picking up women. There was a lot more to Lix Club, there were private rooms and a pool and a dungeon where you could play, but none of that was Genevieve's style. She preferred to pick up women there and take them elsewhere. Genevieve got a drink the moment she sat down and drained it before ordering another that she sipped at a more sedate pace.

She let her eyes rove over the semi-darkened room. There were several possibilities. Her gaze snagged on a tall, pale woman with dark hair that framed her heart-shaped face perfectly, hanging just to her shoulders.

Genevieve felt her mouth popping open. She was probably the most attractive woman Genevieve had ever seen. She knew she was staring like an idiot and forced her eyes back to her drink in case the woman looked over. She looked much younger than Genevieve herself, but then that was Genevieve's thing- hot younger women.

As she sipped on her drink, Genevieve surveyed the woman from beneath her lashes, trying to determine from her behavior if she was even gay. If she wasn't, that would put a stop to the fantasies racing through Genevieve's head rather quickly. But, they usually were in Lix Club. The curious ones weren't Genevieve's cup of tea. She liked women who knew what they wanted and weren't afraid to ask for it.

After ten minutes—the time it took her to finish her drink—Genevieve had determined that the woman was indeed gay, at least by her judgment, and her judgment was usually good. The looks she was giving the other women in the bar were decidedly lesbianny.

She was slim with bright green eyes that seemed to shine when she smiled at the bartender, thanking her for her drink.

Genevieve made her move as the woman finished her next drink, sidling over and signaling the bartender. "I'll buy this one."

The woman blushed as she turned to face Genevieve. "Thank you." She ran her eyes quickly down Genevieve's body before looking back up into her eyes. "I'm Mia."

"Genevieve." Genevieve made to shake hands, but Mia kissed her on the cheek instead.

Forward. I like it.

"It's a pleasure to meet you, Genevieve," she purred.

Despite her easy manner, Genevieve got the strong impression that Mia was holding something back. A shiver of doubt went through her. Though she looked completely different, Mia had a similar air to her as Kate. Genevieve was sure there was some rocky past she was hiding.

She did her best not to think of Kate. That would certainly kill her libido very quickly.

"So, what is a beauty like you doing in a place like this?"

Mia chuckled, though a shadow passed behind her eyes so quickly that Genevieve barely picked it up. "Well, I wanted a drink, and drinking alone is just sad, so I came here. I like being around like-minded women."

"Well, you may be in a bar, but you're still technically alone here. I could keep you company, if you'd like. In the name of not looking sad."

Mia's smile widened. "Well, I'd hate to ruin someone else's good time here by making them witness my sad solo drinking. I suppose you'll have to stay."

Genevieve signaled the bartender for another drink and took a dainty sip.

"I might ask you the same question. You seem to know your way around this place pretty well."

"I'm something of a regular. At least, I usually am. Work has been crazy recently. I figured this is a good night to unwind."

"I like the sound of that."

"Yeah? You look like you could use some stress relief yourself."

"I *have* had a stressful day," Mia said slowly, her eyes sparkling as she pretended to consider. "What did you have in mind?"

"How about you come back to my place and I'll show you."

"Now there's an offer I can't refuse."

Genevieve had to admit, this was going to be good for her ego, which had taken a bit of a hit when she failed to close that deal. There was nothing like a beautiful woman crying out her name and coming on her fingers or tongue to help her feel better about herself.

They finished their drinks, and Genevieve led Mia out of the bar. She enjoyed the undeniable electricity between them as she took Mia's hand. She enjoyed her long graceful fingers and imagined what talents those fingers would show her when they got home.

Genevieve loved this bit. This part with

someone new, beautiful and unknown -where the evening held all this promise and excitement.

Mia's green eyes flashed knowingly. Genevieve had a good feeling about this one. She looked more than a little wild and there was nothing Genevieve enjoyed more than a wild one in the bedroom.

The bartender, Chelsea, winked at her as she went. Chelsea knew all about her escapades here and had even occasionally acted as her wing-woman, when her boss wasn't around.

Genevieve was practically vibrating with excitement. She couldn't believe she had landed a woman like Mia so easily tonight. Sometimes women were so complex and usually picking up a woman for a bit of fun was more of a challenge than Mia had so far proven. Also, it didn't hurt that Mia was absolutely stunning.

She held the door of her car open for Mia, who brushed a hand against Genevieve's hip as she got into the car. That light touch sent tingles through Genevieve's body, a sure promise of what was to come.

Genevieve wasn't a fan of awkward silences during these drives, so she had her small talk ready. However, she found that she wasn't interested in small talk. For some reason, she wanted to know more about Mia as a person.

"What brings you here, Mia? Really?" There seemed to be so much going on behind Mia's eyes. She spoke very little, but her eyes held all this mystery that Genevieve for some reason couldn't resist poking at.

Mia's expression became guarded. "I already told you."

Genevieve quickly backtracked. "I mean, you don't have to talk about it if you don't want to. I just meant that sometimes it helps to vent to a stranger —someone you're never going to see again. I won't bite, I promise... unless asked." She winked at Mia.

Mia chuckled. "Personal issues, I guess. I'm not ready to go home and face the nightmares just yet. Sometimes, being with someone helps. I'm single and I enjoy sex. If I can exhaust myself with a beautiful woman before bed, it helps to keep the nightmares away."

Genevieve was intrigued, but she didn't want to push too far. "Well, I can help in that regard. You have a very thorough fucking coming your way, I can promise you that much," she growled. Genevieve felt hungry at the thought and it was all she could do to keep her hands on the steering wheel. She contemplated reaching a hand over to venture up Mia's skirt as they drove, but decided against it. As fun as it would be, Genevieve knew from experience how distracting hot wet pussy was while driving.

Instead she chose not so subtle glances over Mia's long pale legs enjoying how short and tight Mia's black leather skirt was and how it had ridden higher as she sat down.

Mia laughed again, a beautiful sound, like bells infused with warmth. "That's what I was hoping for. I want you to fuck me so hard I see stars and squirt in every room of your home." They both laughed. Genevieve felt desire rising within her. Fucking Mia was promising to be a pleasure she was going to enjoy every second of.

How old was Mia? Late 20s?

"How old are you, Mia?"

"I'm 28. Will that be a problem for you?"

Fuck, what is it about these hot horny 28 year olds?

Genevieve at 42, knew she was developing a pattern in the women she kept picking up at Lix Club, but who cared? Life was too short to not do what you enjoyed, right?

"Certainly not," she responded. "Fucking 28 year olds is my absolute favorite. Making younger women come over and over on my fingers is the sweetest pleasure," Genevieve growled.

She looked over at Mia's breasts in their low cut shirt. She couldn't wait to see what Mia looked like naked. This was going to be fun.

"What about you?" Mia asked. "Since we're being honest with each other... Why are you picking up horny younger women for sex?"

"Work problems," Genevieve admitted. She wasn't usually open with strangers about her problems, but she had asked Mia to confide in her, after all. The least she could do was be honest in return."

"How predictable," Mia said, drily. Her voice flitted from candy sweet to snarky and dry.

"You'd better watch your tongue, or I might withdraw that thorough fucking I promised you."

"Well, I wouldn't want that." Mia's eyes sparkled in the dark as she pretended to consider. "I suppose you'd better tell me about your work problems, and I'll do my best interested face and that way we will both get what we want this evening."

Genevieve felt desperate to stop the car and fuck her there and then but unfortunately the city wasn't the best place for this. She imagined screeching to a halt, dragging Mia out of the car on a busy city street and throwing her face down over the hood.

She imagined pushing that tight leather skirt up over her ass and ripping her panties right off her. She knew she would be dripping wet.

She imagined fucking her there and then with her fingers bent over the car. She would fuck her hard and without mercy, pounding her G spot until she squirted everywhere.

Then she would leave her there, exposed with her own pleasure running down the inside of her thighs.

Mmmm. Fuck.

Ok, not yet. Patience, Genevieve, patience. Good things come to lesbians who wait.

Something, perhaps unresolved lust or perhaps something else, made Genevieve suddenly want to be honest with this hot stranger.

"As you say, work problems are common and predictable. I'm a CEO and it's a lot of pressure. I'm running my family business and while my parents have always been supportive, they're hard on me. I just failed to land a big business deal, and even at my age, I'm not looking forward to having to tell my father."

"Will he be angry?" Mia's question seemed genuine.

"No, but he'll be disappointed, which in many ways is worse."

Mia hummed her understanding. "That must be difficult."

"Some days, I wish I had followed my brother's example. He said screw it to family expectations and went into the arts. He's a successful painter now."

"Really? I'm a painter as well."

Now this was a subject Genevieve could converse on. Despite the issues between Sean and their parents, she had always been close to her brother.

"What style do you paint in?"

"Usually realism, though I've dabbled in abstract."

"Sean does abstract. I don't understand the meaning behind half of his works, but they're beautiful."

"I liked abstract, and I learned a lot from it, but my true passion is in realism. I travel when I can to get inspiration for different paintings—usually nature-related. I've done mountains, waterfalls, forests, etc. I went to Mount Everest, Niagara Falls, and the Amazon Rainforest. I'm planning to go to the Seychelles to get some ocean inspiration next year."

"You must sell your art for a lot of money to be able to travel so often and widely."

Mia shrugged. "It's less about talent and more about getting your work visible."

"I know the truth of that. Sean has been very lucky that he has family to back him up. My parents didn't accept his choice at first, and he struggled for a few years, but when I started working, I helped him fund some campaigns to get his work noticed. When my parents saw that he truly could make a successful career in his chosen field, they became a lot less judgmental and a lot more supportive."

"That's really great. My parents... well, my father died when I was young, and my mother isn't in the picture anymore."

Genevieve was curious to know more. The haunted look passed behind Mia's eyes again, but her face was once more closed off. She clearly didn't want to talk about family.

"Which gallery do you display your work at?"

"Mostly Elite Artworks, but I also have some pieces at Standford's Gallery and Lily's Collection."

Genevieve raised an eyebrow. "You must be good. I remember how ecstatic Sean was when he got one of his works displayed at Standford's. Elite Artworks is a dream of his."

"The key to their hearts is sincerity. They aren't interested in works that aren't rooted in deeply personal issues."

Genevieve wondered what Mia's deeply personal issues were and made a mental note to visit Elite Artworks and check out some of her paintings.

She was surprised to be confronted suddenly with her driveway. The trip had gone quickly, and she found herself almost wishing it could have gone longer so that she could continue talking to Mia.

Almost.

She let her eyes scan Mia's curves once more and she felt bolts of desire between her legs. Enough of the talking, she was looking forward to what they were about to do too much to be truly disappointed that the moment they would get to fuck was nearly here.

She led Mia inside, flipping on lights as she went. "Can I get you a drink?"

"I think I've had enough to drink tonight. I'm

looking forward to dessert." Mia gave Genevieve a seductive smile as she stepped closer. Genevieve had no objection to moving toward what she truly wanted immediately.

She put a hand on the small of Mia's back, drawing her in. Their lips brushed together, lightly at first and then more firmly. She flicked her tongue out to taste Mia, coming away with the tantalizing taste of mint, spice, and something else she couldn't quite name.

Mia let her mouth open a little, and Genevieve took advantage of the invitation at once, diving into Mia's mouth with her tongue. Mia's tongue snaked forward in return, exploring Genevieve as thoroughly as Genevieve was exploring her.

Mia moaned into the kiss, the sound sending a bolt of lust through Genevieve's body. She could feel her panties quickly becoming soaked, that is if they weren't already from her filthy thoughts on the car ride, this super wetness wasn't a reaction she wasn't used to this early on. Just making out with Mia was making her so horny it was difficult to think clearly.

Genevieve ran her hands down Mia's sides and then back up, coming up to cup her breasts. Mia pulled back just enough to whisper encouragement and pull her own shirt over her head.

Mia clearly was a woman who knew what she wanted and that was absolutely fine with Genevieve.

Their lips met again the moment the shirt was off.

They kissed passionately, frantically. It was clear from the way Mia kissed her back that Mia wanted Genevieve as much as Genevieve wanted her. The thought of such a divine creature desiring her had Genevieve panting harshly for breath as she pulled Mia even closer.

Genevieve reached around Mia's back to unfasten her black lace bra, letting her breasts spring free. She ripped it off her and threw it to the floor. Mia's breasts were larger than she had imagined with big pink nipples.

Fucking beautiful.

It was going to be a good night.

She rubbed her fingers over Mia's nipples, feeling them harden to big tight buds under her touch. Genevieve was finally compelled to withdraw from kissing Mia's lips so that she could get her mouth on her nipples.

She flicked her tongue lightly against one

nipple, testing the reaction. Mia grabbed her hair and guided her mouth onto the nipple, making Genevieve grin before she pulled it into her mouth, sucking deeply.

There was nothing quite like sucking hard on a beautiful woman's tits. Genevieve had missed this. It had been too long. Her body was making violent demands of her, but she was so enjoying Mia's soft sighs of pleasure that she ignored her own needs for now.

She would usually take her partners to the bedroom, but she didn't think they were going to make it there. Genevieve set her eyes on the sofa, backing Mia toward it and roughly pushing her down. She straddled Mia's hips, finally getting some relief as she ground herself down.

"Yeah, just like that," Mia panted. "Let me touch you."

Genevieve stripped off her top and bra, then got off briefly to do the same with her pants and panties. Mia took advantage of the small separation, wriggling out of her own clothes, displaying her body to Genevieve in its full naked glory.

Genevieve moaned as she got back atop Mia, grinding her clit down over Mia's pussy. She was sure she was getting the spot and angle just right, because Mia grabbed her hips and started moving urgently in time with Genevieve.

Genevieve could probably come just like this, but she wanted more. She wanted to taste Mia. She pushed herself further down, but before she could get to what she truly wanted, Mia tapped her hip.

"Flip around. 69.I want my mouth on your pussy too."

"Oh fuck, yes please."

Genevieve positioned herself so that Mia could reach her. She felt Mia's tongue flick lightly over her clit and murmured her encouragement before doing the same for Mia.

It was difficult to concentrate when Mia's tongue was working its magic on her. Mia was clearly perceptive and quickly learned which touches Genevieve liked—soft, almost ticklish licks, followed up by one long, firmer one before reverting to soft and ticklish again. She repeated the pattern, driving Genevieve wild with need.

Well, Mia wasn't the only one who could be perceptive. Genevieve was well-versed in picking up her partner's needs. She propped herself up on one elbow so that she could gently tease Mia's entrance with a finger. Mia reacted by widening her legs further, an obvious invitation.

Genevieve pushed two fingers inside her, wriggling her wrist around so she could curl them up at Mia's G spot. As soon as she hit it, Mia arched up and cried out, momentarily releasing Genevieve's clitoris from her mouth. The short break only made it that much sweeter when Mia got back to work on her.

Genevieve pushed relentlessly on Mia's G-spot while finally spreading her folds and seeking out her clitoris with her tongue. Mia's clit was there, ready and waiting for attention. Genevieve gave it an experimental lick, waiting for Mia's reaction. Mia did not disappoint, gasping and jerking into the touch.

Genevieve soon learned that Mia responded best to long, firm licks, repeated with no variation while she fucked her rhythmically with her fingers. Genevieve was only too happy to give her exactly what she wanted. Mia was letting out small, desperate little whimpers. Though her tongue was too busy for her to speak, Genevieve was sure that she was nearing her release.

Genevieve pulled back a little, easing up with her tongue. She wanted to come at the same time as Mia. Such a thing was tricky to work at the best of times, but this was definitely the best of times.

Genevieve was enjoying this easy chemistry with a stranger all too much. Genevieve put a hand on Mia's hip when Mia tried to move forward, desperate for more.

"Wait," she murmured. "I'm so—oh God—so close, Mia. We'll do this together. Tell me you have a thing for older women grinding on your face."

Mia didn't hesitate and moaned in answer, "I love hot older women grinding their pussy on my face while they fuck me...I want to taste your orgasm, I want you to flood my mouth with your come until I drown in you..." the sound of her words for sure was sending Genevieve over the edge.

Genevieve felt her thighs start to tighten as the pleasure began to peak. She went back to Mia's clit with a vengeance, giving her the firm pressure she needed as her fingers thrust harder.

It worked perfectly. Genevieve's orgasm hit her hard, and it was all she could do to keep going on Mia's clit. She wasn't sure if her movements were perfect anymore, but whether or not she was getting it exactly how she wanted it didn't seem to matter, because Mia was coming too.

Genevieve felt a surge of wetness around her fingers as Mia clenched around her. She thrust her fingers in and out a few times as Mia squirted wildly, her body shaking as her own pleasure roared through her.

Oh fuck, yes...

Genevieve's expensive sofa was getting squirted on, but she really didn't care. Fucking Mia while she came on her face was so much fun. Exactly the release she needed.

Genevieve was still coming. Over and over as she ground down on Mia's face. Her orgasm went on and on, longer than it ever had before. She removed her mouth from Mia and sat upright to get every last bit of pleasure. She kept her fingers inside Mia and watched as she fucked her more and harder and Mia just squirted more and harder. It was spraying out of her pussy.

How was it possible for anyone to squirt this much?

Genevieve felt herself building again as Mia took her clitoris in her mouth and sucked hard.

"Oh fuck, oh, Mia. Jesus. That feels so good."

Genevieve watched as Mia's legs opened further as if wordlessly begging for more fucking.

It was a slightly awkward angle but Genevieve was enjoying it too much to stop. She added a third finger and thrust into Mia as hard as she could.

She felt the sucking on her clitoris intensify and just when she thought it wasn't possible to come any more her mind and body flooded with pleasure from what felt like her 24th orgasm of the evening.

As she came back to earth she saw Mia's hips rising slightly and heard her murmur.

"Please, uh, I'm so close, again. Put your thumb to my clitoris while you fuck me. Please..."

It was an easy adjustment. Genevieve moved her thumb to Mia's clitoris giving her the pressure she had clearly been craving.

Seconds later, she watched as Mia's body writhed in ecstasy tightening and releasing in the throes of orgasm. She cried out loudly into Genevieve's pussy.

Fuck. Who is this woman?

Genevieve extracted her fingers finally and fell back down to the big expansive sofa that was now soaked in Mia's juices.

Hmmm. Going to have to get that cleaned professionally, but never mind. That was incredible.

They both lay there, panting, recovering from what Genevieve suddenly realized was the best sex she'd ever had. Even with Kate...

Don't think about that.

She wasn't going to ruin this beautiful moment with such morbid thoughts. She was too blissed-out to allow that to happen. Genevieve instead flipped herself around so that she and Mia could entangle themselves in each other's arms. Genevieve kissed Mia almost chastely, a kiss that Mia returned languidly for a few moments before tucking her head into Genevieve's shoulder, sighing contentedly.

"I certainly struck it lucky tonight. That was incredible," Mia murmured.

"You've taken the words right out of my mouth."

They lay in strangely comfortable silence for a while. Genevieve usually struggled with these silences. She didn't like to kick her partners out the moment they were finished, but this also seemed an inappropriate time to resume with the small talk.

However, with Mia, she was perfectly content to lie here, feeling Mia's heartbeat through her palm, which was pressed against Mia's back.

Genevieve began to wonder if Mia was drifting off, something she usually didn't allow in one night stands, though she suspected she would make an exception here. It had been the best sex of her life, after all, and she was in a mood to make allowances.

However, Mia stirred and pushed herself up, seemingly reluctantly. Her dark hair fell loosely around her pretty face and her green eyes seemed much more relaxed and peaceful than they had earlier. "I should go. I have a showing tomorrow afternoon. I want to get at least some sleep."

Genevieve nodded and got up as well. She handed Mia her clothes and watched as Mia got dressed. There was an easy elegance to Mia's beautiful pale naked body, almost like a dancer. Every movement she made seemed fluid and full of grace.

Genevieve enjoyed watching Mia's breasts sway and seeing the swell of her nipples- still such a turn on. She enjoyed the roundness of Mia's ass as she bent over to pull her lace panties on.

Definitely should have found time to fuck her from behind.

Mia was really beautiful.

Mmm. Some nice images to keep in my head to remind me of tonight.

"Good luck for your showing tomorrow. I really hope it goes well."

"Thanks, Genevieve. I hope your father isn't too hard on you."

"I'll figure it out." Genevieve hesitated, wanting to prolong the moment when Mia had to leave—her company was just so *easy* for some reason, a far cry from many of the one-night stands Genevieve had had. Very few people had looks like Mia's and the personality to back that up and also the ease of enjoying sex for what it was and not complicating pleasure with emotion.

"Well, goodbye, then."

As always, the goodbyes were slightly awkward, but it was part of the price Genevieve paid, and for that sex, she would gladly have paid a much higher one.

"Bye, Mia. All the best."

"To you as well."

Genevieve let Mia out and locked the door behind her before practically skipping to bed, except her body was too lax and relaxed to skip properly.

This night had turned out way better than she ever could have hoped. She was definitely ending the day on a high note, and all thoughts of business were, if not gone, at least postponed until the morning. Genevieve would clean up the mess on the couch later. Or get a professional in. Probably the latter.

She fell into bed but didn't fall asleep immediately. She found her mind wandering to Mia. They seemed to have formed an instant connection, something Genevieve wasn't used to. Ever since Kate, she had been unwilling to open her heart to anyone. She was not going through that kind of pain again.

Genevieve kept a tight schedule, for the most part keeping herself too busy to feel lonely. Some nights, she felt the void in her personal life. She had to admit that it was a bit extreme to push even friendships away, but she maintained that personal entanglements led to pain. When you loved someone, there was always pain.

It was better this way. She found pleasure when she wanted it and brought pleasure to her partners. It was perhaps not what other people approved of—the idea that you had to be in a relationship to be happy was widespread and false—but it worked for her. For the most part.

Genevieve finally drifted off, and her sleep was graced by pleasant dreams of ivory skin and green eyes.

2

MIA

Mia Spencer took an uber back to Lix Club to pick up her car. She was positively giddy, tipping big and waving cheerily at the driver as she sauntered to her car.

She had simply gone to Lix Club to get blind drunk and forget. She had been on her way to doing just that when the opportunity of a night with a beautiful stranger had presented itself. Mia had seldom been so glad that she'd taken an opportunity. That sex had been eye-opening, to say the least.

Mia had had sex before, but it paled in comparison to what she had shared with

Genevieve. She wondered if it was common to find someone that compatible with her, or if it was as rare for Genevieve as it was for her.

It had quickly become clear that Genevieve was experienced in the art of picking up strangers and taking them home. Mia wondered why that was. A woman like Genevieve who was beautiful and enigmatic and clearly very wealthy should have no problem finding partners for a real relationship.

Mia could only conclude that this simply wasn't what Genevieve was looking for. That was fine, of course. Mia felt like she ultimately needed a true partner in life to feel fulfilled, but she wasn't arrogant enough to believe that everyone else had that same need.

She got home and fell into bed, still slightly dazed from earlier. Perhaps, tonight, she would sleep without nightmares. She had certainly gotten the thorough fucking Genevieve had promised her. Hopefully, it would be enough.

Unfortunately, though it had undoubtedly been the best sex of her life, it turned out not to be enough.

Mia woke with a start at around two a.m., covered in cold sweat. She sat up in bed, sighing as the images bombarded her. She had been five when her father died in a car crash and ten when her mother remarried.

Her mother had been deeply in love with her stepfather, but for Mia, it was far from the happy picture her mother painted. Silas started off okay... until he started drinking. He got nasty when he was drunk. Very nasty.

Mia wasn't an idiot. She knew what PTSD was. She knew that abuse survivors everywhere recovered and lived without the shadow of their past hanging over them. Mia was scared, though. She didn't want to open up to a stranger about her deepest, darkest secrets. Seeking treatment would make her vulnerable in a way she hadn't been since she was sixteen.

As always, the thought brought on a wave of bitterness. When Mia had finally worked up the courage to confront her mother, her mother took Silas' side. Mia knew, then, that waiting and hoping for the situation to get better was never going to work.

Mia had never regretted running away at sixteen. Even during her lowest times in the shelters, before she was earning enough money from her paintings to get her own place, it was a thousand times better than what she had left behind.

She was dwelling on it, again. Mia forced herself out of bed and to her home studio. Painting always soothed her. Hopefully she could still get a few hours of sleep.

She let her thread of inspiration guide her. Mia seldom painted people, but after tonight, she felt an urge to do so. She sketched an outline, becoming immersed in the work. The woman didn't look exactly like Genevieve, but encapsulated her beauty, poise and competent air.

Mia had to force herself to stop when her eyes began itching with tiredness. She stumbled back to bed and pulled the covers up over her head.

Thankfully, this time, she slept without nightmares.

The next day, Mia arrived early to her showing. It was an important one. A representative from the creative department of some bigshot investment company, Wisdom Investments, was coming to see her work. If he liked it, he would recommend that the CEO come and meet with her personally.

Mia knew that this kind of opportunity could be career-changing for her. She knew that her work was good, but even being known in the local arts scene, getting visibility was always a problem. If she could just get her work out there, she knew she had the potential to expand her career so much more, maybe even becoming known internationally.

Mia had selected some of the paintings showed in Elite Artworks to bring to the showing, but she had also painted one with this meeting specifically in mind. Mia usually painted nature, but she had occasionally done city scenes before. This painting was a view of the city lights at night, with the shadow of a mountain in the background.

She was extremely pleased with it and thought it would appeal to such business-minded people more than a waterfall or a mountain, no matter how skillfully executed.

Mia was early for the meeting, ready to wait, but the representative arrived exactly on time.

"Hi, Mia, I'm Archer, from Wisdom Investments. I've heard a lot of good things about you and your work."

"Thank you. It's an honor to receive interest from an organization like yours."

Mia was eager to get straight to showing him her work, but she recognized the unfortunate need for small talk. "Please, tell me more about your department."

"Well, one of our specialties is investing in talent, nurturing it and turning it into something truly spectacular. It's not like other companies, where the higher-ups stifle their creative staff, wanting only profit. They want profit, to be sure, but we're given freedom to work, and help achieving that aim where necessary."

That certainly sounded hopeful, though Mia would need to be sure of some more specifics before she arranged any kind of deal. She certainly wasn't going to give up her independence to work in an office, but she was sure that she could come to some arrangement with their CEO if her work passed inspection.

"What about you? What inspires you to paint?"

It was something she was always asked, and something Mia had found very difficult to answer at first, but she had been through this so many times that she rolled her answer out by rote without thinking about it much.

"I've had a troubled past, with lots of ugliness. Painting things of beauty brings me peace and joy. I love to find the wonder in things I see and imagine and bring them to life to inspire others."

"That does sound inspiring. I'd love to see some of your work."

"Of course. Please, follow me."

Mia had spent an hour making sure the lighting in the showing room was just right. She held out an arm in invitation, indicating for Archer to go ahead of her.

He stepped slowly into the room, his eyes roving over the paintings. Unsurprisingly, he went to the city one first. "Truly spectacular," he murmured. "I see they didn't exaggerate your talent. What gave you the inspiration for this one?"

"I travel for work sometimes, and I always take photos when I see something striking. I refer back to those to remind myself of what I saw and how I felt, then I take that as inspiration for my paintings. This particular one was taken in Denver. It's not exactly like the photo—I took some artistic license—but the feeling of it is the same."

"Beautiful. I see it's not much like your other works."

"That's right—I usually go for natural scenes. It's sometimes nice to do something different, though. It keeps things interesting."

Archer nodded as he moved over to a painting of a magnificent waterfall. Mia remembered how long it had taken her to get the foam just right and was pleased to see him eyeing it appreciatively.

"I see you work under the name Illuven. Does that have any particular meaning?"

"I kind of made it up. It comes loosely from Eru Ilúvatar, from *Lord of the Rings*. The sound of it evokes images of light for me. It was just a silly pen name at first, something I thought I'd test out to see how my early works did. I didn't want to work under my real name in the beginning. If I didn't do well under Illuven, I could easily change to another nickname. However, I did well as Illuven and saw no reason to change it."

"That's an interesting story. Stuff like that adds depth to your profile as an artist. Have you ever explained it formally?"

"No, but I've never really had occasion I don't have enough of a fanbase yet to release formal statements."

"Well, hopefully we can change that."

Archer asked a few more questions, but mostly, he just appreciated the artwork. Mia could tell that he was impressed, but was he impressed enough to recommend her to his undoubtedly very busy boss?

"Thank you, Mia, this has been most enlightening. I understand that you're part of Elite Artworks' exhibition next week?"

"That's right."

"I'm going to tell our CEO in no uncertain terms that she needs to be there."

Mia resisted the urge to whoop and leap into the air. Instead, she smiled at Archer, hoping she didn't come off as giddy as she felt. "Thank you, Archer. I look forward to meeting your CEO."

"Thank you, Mia. This has truly been a treat. All the best—I hope to be working with you soon."

Mia was too excited to settle into anything when she got home. She eventually gave up on work and went for a walk. She snapped a great photo of a puppy playing in the autumn leaves, vaguely thinking of doing a painting replacing the sidewalk around it with a soft forest floor.

When she got home, she was finally able to work.

Mia was working on one more painting for the exhibition, which was almost finished—a vibrant green jungle. As much as she liked the painting, she wasn't feeling inspired to work on it right now. She was drawn to the painting she had started last night—the one of the strong, capable woman with eyes that seemed to see right through her and the body of a goddess.

She was lying on her side in a field of brightly colored flowers at dawn, completely naked. Her hair was spread out behind her and her face lit by the rising sun.

Usually, it would be difficult to perfect a painting like this in a week, but when Mia felt fired up with inspiration like she did now, she could easily work for fifteen hours a day on it. Of course, she couldn't maintain that kind of thing for long, but after the exhibition, things should calm down.

It would likely be some time before the investors got back to her—they would need to discuss it with their various committees—and Mia would have time to relax before hopefully diving into her next venture.

She painted late into the night, and for the first time in about three months, she had a night free of nightmares. She instead saw beautiful women among flowers, beckoning for her to join them.

Mia did.

3

GENEVIEVE

Genevieve was excited for the exhibition. Archer had scoped out a number of potential talented artists, though he was most excited about one who went under the name Illuven. Genevieve had seen some samples of her work and was eager to see them in person.

She had even sent a few to Sean, who had confirmed that the artist was very talented—in fact someone he had already heard of and followed.

Genevieve wandered through the gallery, having a look at what was on offer. Waiters were serving wine from trays, and she took a glass, sipping daintily on it as she surveyed the room. She soon came to a small section labeled *Illuven*.

Genevieve was immediately drawn in by a stunning painting of a city at night, backed by the shadow of a mountain. The lights were so bright and so real that it made her feel like she was really there. She resisted the urge to touch the painting, knowing that artists took a dim view of strangers feeling up their work.

"Is this painting for sale?" Genevieve turned to the woman who she assumed was the artist and choked on her sip of wine.

It was Mia. Genevieve's most recent one night stand.

Mia's expression displayed similar shock. "Genevieve?"

"Mia." Genevieve coughed a few times. "*You're* Illuven?"

"That's right. Did you come to see my work?"

Mia didn't recognize who she was. Perhaps she thought Genevieve had simply been curious after their discussion that night last week.

"Yes. We never got properly introduced. I'm Genevieve Mitchell, CEO of Wisdom Investments."

Now, it was Mia's turn to nearly choke. She went bright red. "I—I didn't know."

"Clearly. Neither did I." Genevieve took a deep breath, centering herself. The fact that they'd had a fantastic one-night stand didn't have to change anything. It all depended on how they handled it.

Genevieve decided not to address the issue for now and focus on business. They would no doubt need to talk about it if they ended up working together, but she wanted to start things on a professional note.

"Is this painting for sale?"

"It is. The ones in this section are for sale. These ones here already belong to various galleries."

There were so many beautiful artworks that Genevieve didn't know where to look. One in particular drew her eye. This time, she was the one to go red.

The nude woman in the painting wasn't Genevieve, but she had enough of Genevieve to make her self-conscious.

"Is this one...?"

"It's inspired by a particularly good night I had with a beautiful stranger." Mia winked at her, and Genevieve found herself blushing harder. It took a lot to tongue-tie her, but she found herself lost for words. It was extremely flattering, being the inspiration for a painting like this.

"It's... it's wonderful."

Mia blushed as well. "I'm glad you think so."

"How much do you want for this city one."

Mia was clearly prepared for the question. She grabbed a notebook that was sitting on one of the short columns spread throughout the room and wrote down a number.

It was an ambitious bid, but the painting was definitely worth it. Genevieve knew that it would be acceptable to haggle in this kind of situation, but she felt the painting was worth the high price.

"I'll take it."

Judging by her look of surprise, Mia had clearly been expecting Genevieve to try to bargain with her.

"Perfect! Thank you, Genevieve."

"Thank *you*, Mia. Now, let's get down to business, shall we? I would like you to come and work for my company."

Mia bit her lip. "No."

Disappointment flooded Genevieve's insides. Perhaps Mia thought it would be too complicated entering a situation where she had slept with her boss. That would be a fair concern, but Genevieve had hoped they could work around it. "You've changed your mind about wanting to work with us, then?"

"Absolutely not. I would love to work with you and your company, Genevieve, but not as an employee. I would like to maintain my independence, but I'm sure we can cut some kind of deal."

It wasn't how Genevieve usually did things. She preferred the talent she fostered to be directly under her wing. She would usually say no outright to such a request. If someone wanted to work with her, they could do it her way; and if not, there were plenty of others who would kill for such an opportunity.

However, she was strongly tempted to make an exception for Mia. Genevieve did a quick scan of her feelings, trying to determine if the fond memories of their encounter last week were interfering with her business sense and her assessment of Mia's talent.

No, she didn't think that was it. Both Sean and Archer had said that Mia was brilliant, and they would know better than Genevieve on the artwork side. Genevieve's job was to assess Mia as a person and decide whether she would be a good fit for the company.

If she wasn't joining the company, that would be a less important question. Genevieve had a good feeling about Mia. She had gotten to know her more intimately than she had ever done with a potential business connection, and the brief time she had spent talking to her had been promising.

In the end, Genevieve decided to trust her gut, which seldom let her down.

"What did you have in mind?"

Mia had her answer ready. "It's simple. You promote my work and I give you a share in the profit from all the paintings I sell. I can offer you fifteen percent."

"Twenty-five," Genevieve offered.

"Twenty," Mia countered.

"Twenty-two."

Mia grinned. "You have yourself a deal."

They shook hands. Genevieve was resisting the urge to go into a victory dance, and she suspected that Mia felt much the same. This going to be a very good deal for both of them. Not only was it sure to be profitable, but Genevieve would get to know Mia better, something she was eager to do.

"I'll have my lawyers draw up the contract today. For now, we should go out to celebrate."

Mia bit her lip again, an action so cute it made

Genevieve long to free that lip with hers. "I should really stay until the end of the exhibition. It wouldn't be professional to leave halfway through."

Working with someone who didn't answer solely to her would certainly be different, but Genevieve was sure she could get used to the idea. Her father probably wouldn't be pleased at first, but once the venture started proving as profitable as Genevieve suspected it would be, his attitude would change fast.

"Of course, I understand. I need to make some calls anyway, as well as set up the transfer for that painting. I want to walk out of here with it. I've already got a space on my wall picked out in my head."

"Perfect. I'd love to join you for drinks after the exhibition is done." Mia handed Genevieve a slip of paper with her bank details on it, as well as the paper with the price they had agreed on.

"I'll be back in a couple of hours, then. I can have the contract printed out and I'll bring it with me."

Genevieve realized that there were probably a lot more questions she should have asked. It wasn't like her to jump straight into a business deal.

However, she also trusted her own judgement, and she was sure that this was going to end well.

She gave the rest of the artwork in the exhibition a few cursory glances, but even though much of it was very good, it paled in comparison to Mia's work.

Genevieve called the company contract lawyer and instructed him to come up with a contract stating the terms she and Mia had agreed on. If he was surprised by this change in business model, he didn't say anything.

Genevieve did the transfer and went back to the office to pick up the contract. She had cleared her whole day for this, thinking she'd spend hours poring through the gallery. However, she had what she came for. Now, she was going to have a well-earned treat.

It was nearly lunchtime, and Genevieve collected all of her employees into the main office. There were a few nervous looks, and Genevieve quickly sought to reassure them. "Good news, I promise. I know that we've all been working hard, and everyone is disappointed that we didn't make that last deal. I want you to know that I don't blame any of you, and there will be plenty more deals in the future. We all deserve a little break. I'm sending you all out to lunch on me, to a place of your choice."

A small cheer broke out, and people immediately started making suggestions for places to go. They settled on a fancy Italian place that Genevieve had been to several times before. Penelope, Genevieve's assistant, immediately started organizing people into cars.

Genevieve would be sure to follow this up with the appropriate financial action. Taking people out to lunch was all well and good, but she knew that if she truly wanted to show her appreciation, she needed to put her money where her mouth was. It had been a while since she'd awarded raises other than the standard annual increase, and this seemed to be a good time to do it.

Jake made his way through the small crowd, holding a thin folder. "Here's that contract you wanted, Genevieve. This new artist must be excellent. You certainly seem in a really good mood."

"I am, but I could have celebrated by taking myself out for ice cream. I meant what I said—you all deserve a break."

"You should join us."

"Yes, join us, Genevieve," Penelope added. Several others echoed her sentiment.

Genevieve was touched by their sincerity, but she didn't need that kind of interaction. She was showing her appreciation well enough; no need to get personal about it.

"I won't be joining today, but you all have fun. I'll come with you to get things sorted with the manager, then I'll leave you to it."

"Come on, Genevieve, life a little," Penelope teased.

"Yeah, yeah, I will. Next time."

She was met with a round of chuckles. She wasn't going to join them next time and they all knew it.

Genevieve made a generous deposit to the restaurant and instructed the manager to send her the final bill. After telling him to treat her staff well and give them anything they wanted, she returned to the empty office. It was still a few hours until she was due to meet Mia.

It wasn't unusual for her to take clients or new colleagues out for a meal or a drink to ease into the relationship. That itself wouldn't raise eyebrows; it was just part of business. Genevieve was glad that no one could see into her head and read exactly how excited she was to get to spend more time with Mia.

She whiled away the hours catching up on some admin. Penelope could have handled it, but Genevieve had time, so she thought she'd make her assistant's life a little easier.

With about an hour to go, Genevieve went home, showered and changed clothes. She didn't know where Mia would want to go, so she wore a versatile outfit—casual, but with a chiffon shawl in her bag that could be draped around her shoulders to make it more appropriate for somewhere fancy.

Mia was waiting for her at the gallery entrance when Genevieve arrived. She gave Genevieve a warm smile and walked up to meet her. She was holding the painting Genevieve had purchased. "Hi. I've got your painting."

"Hi, Mia. Thank you; it truly is lovely. I have the contact here. Do you have an idea of where you want to go?"

"Anywhere you'd like. I don't often do this kind of thing, and I'm not sure where would be appropriate."

"Fabiola is a good place for these kinds of celebrations. Great drinks, and some snack food if you're hungry."

"That sounds great."

Genevieve experienced no small amount of déjà vu while leading Mia to her car. The last time had been under entirely different circumstances, but both situations had one thing in common: Genevieve was sure it was going to end well for both parties.

She put the painting carefully in her trunk, positioning it so that it wouldn't get jostled during the ride.

The upscale bar was already busy, but Genevieve took one of the booths with a table, which was quieter and more private.

"Business first, I think. Here's the contract. If you'd like to have your lawyer take a look at it…"

"No, I can read it for myself. Legal jargon doesn't scare me."

Genevieve was sure that Mia would reconsider when reading the contract. It wasn't deliberately complex, but picking through legal terms was usually difficult for artists like Mia, who were more creative than analytical.

However, Mia seemed to have little trouble with it. Her brow made the most adorable concentration furrow as she read. She asked a few questions, but Genevieve read comprehension and—

even more attractively—intelligence in her face as her eyes followed the writing on the papers.

"That seems fair—exactly what we agreed on. I'm happy to sign this." Genevieve was about to offer a pen, but Mia came up with her own and signed the contract. She handed it over to Genevieve, who added her name.

"Perfect. I'll have a certified copy made and sent to you tomorrow. I'd love to see more of your work sometime."

The drinks arrived and Mia raised hers in a toast. "To our new partnership."

Genevieve did the same. "To our partnership. May it be long and fruitful."

4

MIA

To say Mia was elated was an understatement. She was ecstatic to have landed an investor as big as Genevieve Mitchell. She had initially thought their one-night stand would complicate things, but Genevieve wasn't acting weird about it, so Mia was determined to do the same.

They toasted and each took a sip.

Genevieve was the first one to broach the subject. "I never imagined that the Illuven Archer spoke about would be you. I got quite a surprise, to say the least."

"You and me both. I knew you were a CEO, but

I had no idea you were running Wisdom Investments."

"Yes, well, my tongue was somewhat occupied the last time we were together."

Mia chuckled and almost choked on her sip of champagne. "Mine as well. How are we going to handle that?"

"We're both adults. I'm sure we can keep the past in the past. It was just a one-night stand. It's a weird coincidence that we're now working together, but I don't see why it should interfere with our business relationship."

Mia was glad that Genevieve took that stance, but she did have a few concerns about her ability to hold up her end of that bargain. If she was being honest with herself, she was practically champing at the bit to get Genevieve back into bed.

Genevieve's black pantsuit was cut perfectly around her body highlighting her curves in a way that meant Mia couldn't take her eyes off them. She wore black Louboutin heels that were super sexy and her hair was an exquisite icy blonde bob. Her eyes were shimmering blue.

Of course, trying to proposition her new investor would be extremely inappropriate, even given their history. Still, Mia couldn't help wondering whether Genevieve would be open to such a development.

The impression Mia got of her was that Genevieve was emotionally reserved, but she wasn't opposed to connecting to others with sex. Mia wondered if Genevieve was only interested in one-night stands, or if she might be open to a more regular arrangement.

Genevieve's voice brought her guiltily out of her thoughts. "I'd love to see where you work sometime—if you're willing to show me, of course."

"It's nothing fancy. I just have a small studio in my house. You're welcome to come and see it if you'd like."

Right now. Naked. With me fucking you on the floor beneath one of my paintings.

Shut up, Mia! That is not *the way to think in a business meeting.*

This wasn't technically a business meeting, but it was close enough. Mia needed to keep her hands to herself if she wanted to keep Genevieve as an investor, as much as she wanted to put them all over Genevieve's body.

"What about you? You know I'm passionate about my work. Do you enjoy yours?" Mia found it difficult to imagine enjoying some boring corporate desk job, but Genevieve certainly seemed invested in it.

Genevieve grinned widely. "I love it! It's amazing seeing what it's possible to build with a little effort and perseverance. It takes time to surround yourself with the best people, but I've got a great staff, and we're all on the same page about the business."

"That must be hard to find."

"Well, it's partially found, partially created. I look for people who are honest, hardworking and talented. Those kinds of things, you just have to keep looking until you find the right people. Once you have the right people, there are some simple ways to keep them motivated."

"Like what?" Mia had never been much interested in business, but Genevieve's enthusiasm had her curious. She hadn't seen Genevieve so animated about anything before, at least in the short time they had known each other.

"Well, one of the things I do is offer them small shares in the company after they have been working for a year. They can buy more shares at a discounted rate. That keeps them invested in the company's success. Other than that, it's just the standard stuff—good wages, good benefits, under-standing as well as firmness. Managing things fairly. Normal business stuff."

"You make it sound easy."

"It's simple in theory. Executing that theory can be easier said than done, but experience gets you a long way in that regard. But enough about me. Tell me what inspires you to paint."

This again. Mia had her standard answer ready. "I have a troubled past. My experiences were a dark blot in my life at one point, and my painting brings me light and peace."

She could stop there, but for some reason, she found herself wanting to confide in Genevieve. "I've been painting since I was... since I was twelve. That was a dark time in my life, and painting really helped me get through."

Genevieve's eyes were burning with curiosity, but she didn't push for more than Mia was willing to give her.

Mia opened her mouth to tell the whole truth but chickened out. She hadn't told anyone since she was sixteen, when she told her mother, and look how that had turned out. Why would Genevieve believe her, if her own mother hadn't?

Besides, they were out celebrating here. No need to share her whole sad life story.

"That must have been quite a rough time."

"It was." Mia decided it was best to change the subject. "What about you? Any past traumas you want to share? If I'm spilling my guts, I expect you to do the same."

Genevieve stiffened.

"I was just joking, Genevieve," Mia quickly assured her. "You don't owe me anything. We're business partners."

Genevieve nodded, getting a hold of herself quickly. She changed the subject again. "I'll talk to our head of marketing tomorrow. Archer is great. He's done a lot of work with the creative department, and he already has some connections in the art world. I'd like to get your work seen at some galleries in other states. Would you be able to do a series for me?"

Mia tried to contain her trepidation. Having her work displayed in another state sounded wonderful, but what exactly would Genevieve expect of her? How much control did she expect to have over what Mia painted? "What type of series?"

"Anything you'd like—just something with a

theme. We can fit the marketing around whatever you choose."

"I can do that." Archer had been telling the truth about being given creative freedom. Excitement replaced anxiety. "I'll have to think about it and send you a proposal in a few days."

"That sounds perfect. Thanks, Mia."

Mia's mind was already spinning with the possibilities. Bright green spring scenes filled with sunshine, to celebrate her joy at having such a good opportunity. Rainbows arcing through the sky, joining one coast to another. Animals in the forest, playing in autumn leaves.

Beautiful, naked women draped over rocks backed by waterfalls, swinging on vine-covered branches and sitting on pristine beaches in the setting sun.

Looking at Genevieve, Mia certainly knew what she was inspired to do right now.

She'd have to write her proposal carefully. Nudity could sometimes be a touchy issue, though it was easy enough to artfully cover certain areas of the body. It was also different to Mia's usual work, and Genevieve may want what she normally did, given that it was what had enticed her into entering this business arrangement in the first place.

Genevieve's voice drew Mia out of her thoughts. "It's getting late. We should probably go."

Mia realized that Genevieve was right. They had finished their third round of drinks already, though Mia had switched to soda after the first one. She had no need to get drunk enough to forget tonight. Tonight, her head was full of pleasant thoughts.

She found that she didn't want the evening to end yet. She was drawn to Genevieve's confidence, her clear intelligence, and the warmth she showed toward Mia. Mia got the impression that it wasn't the way she usually acted around people, though she would have to see more of Genevieve's interactions to be sure on that point.

"Would you like to come and see my studio? I mean, I know it's late, so if you need to go—"

"No, I'd love to see your studio! I've only ever been in Sean's studio before. It'll be really interesting to see another artist's haunt."

"Great." Mia was nervous again. How would her little studio compare to Sean's? Maybe his was big and fancy. He had people with money backing him up, after all. Mia did well with her art, but there was only so much space in her house for a studio, and she liked her home. She wasn't in a hurry to upgrade from something comforting and familiar to something that would seem cold and empty, at least at first.

Genevieve insisted on paying, and Mia directed her through to the streets, right to her house. Mia led the way in, taking Genevieve to the lounge first. "Would you like a drink?"

"I think I've had enough for tonight. And I'm eager to see your studio."

Mia had been hoping for a chance to sit and talk a while longer. She really enjoyed talking to Genevieve. However, Genevieve was a busy woman and Mia didn't want to delay her if she needed to go.

"This way, then."

Mia shot a nervous glance at Genevieve as they entered the studio. Genevieve's face displayed open curiosity. She smiled as she walked among the paintings, her keen eyes taking in every detail.

"This is wonderful. It's where you come to relax?" Her eyes went to the beanbag in the corner with a little coffee table next to it.

"Yeah, that's right. It's where I do my work, and

my work has always been a solace. Sometimes, if I'm... stressed... I come in here and read for a bit, or just sip on some tea."

"It must be nice, to have a place like that."

"You don't?" Mia would have thought that with a job a stressful as Genevieve's was bound to be, a sanctuary would be essential.

"I've just never really set anything up. I mean, I suppose I could, but when would I spend time there? I'm always at work. Home is only really for sleeping."

That sounded awful, but Mia didn't say so. If it worked for Genevieve, that was none of her business, but she couldn't help noting the tinge of sadness in Genevieve's tone.

"Well, for me, home is for comfort, and a safe place. For work, too, clearly, but that's not a mutually exclusive concept."

"Your paintings really are beautiful... almost as beautiful as their creator."

Mia felt herself blushing. She wondered once again whether Genevieve would be open to more between them. It would be unorthodox, to be sure, but that didn't mean they couldn't make it work.

"You know, I meant it when I said you inspired that one back at the gallery."

"Oh, I know. I was kind of embarrassed seeing other people look at it."

"Was it too close?" Mia was suddenly concerned. "I tried to make it different enough that it didn't look exactly like you."

"It wasn't exactly like me," Genevieve admitted. "It was fairly close, but I'm not unhappy about that. It's flattering, knowing that I inspire someone like you."

"Your mind and your body," Mia murmured. Screw the proposal. If she could use her idea to get Genevieve into bed, she was going to give it a shot. "You know, I was thinking of doing something along those lines for the series. What do you think?"

"What do I think of beautiful naked women? Do you even have to ask?"

"Well in that case... I'd better make this series one of my best. I want to do well by both of us."

"I'm sure you will."

"A little extra inspiration couldn't hurt, though."

"Oh yeah?" Genevieve unbuttoned the top three buttons of her shirt. "Inspiration like this?"

"Exactly like that," Mia murmured. "May I?"

"Who am I to stand in the way of an artist's inspiration? I'm yours."

Mia's heart and body roared in triumph as she finally got her hands on Genevieve. She unbuttoned the rest of the shirt with trembling fingers, finally pulling it back off Genevieve's shoulders. Genevieve was wearing a practical beige bra, but it was what was underneath the bra that truly interested Mia.

She hadn't gotten an opportunity to explore Genevieve's breasts last time. She certainly wanted Genevieve's pussy, but this time, she wanted the breasts in the bargain.

"Here." Mia led Genevieve to the beanbag and the two of them lay down. Mia took one breast in each hand and stroked them, rubbing her thumbs over the nipples.

Genevieve leaned forward and kissed her, slowly at first, but the kiss soon heated up. The beanbag squashed beneath them as Genevieve changed her angle, reaching up under Mia's dress, trailing up her thigh to brush over her panties.

Those panties were currently in the process of getting thoroughly damp. Mia broke away to gasp for air as Genevieve wormed a hand inside her panties and parted her folds to touch her clit.

Genevieve used the break in the kiss to start

trailing wet kisses down Mia's neck. The angle brought her breasts away from Mia, which Mia wasn't thrilled about, but she was so focused on Genevieve's fingers, rubbing lightly and rhythmically on her clit, that it was difficult to concentrate on anything else.

Mia realized that if she wasn't careful, she was going to come before she'd gotten what she wanted.

"Clothes off," she murmured, pleased when Genevieve immediately obliged her. She used the brief break in contact to try to gather her scattered mind.

She wanted all of Genevieve, and she wanted her right now. Mia slotted one of her legs between Genevieve's, rolling on top of her and bringing her mouth to one of Genevieve's nipples.

Genevieve moaned softly and turned slightly to give Mia a better angle.

Mia was lost in the erotic sensation of sucking on Genevieve's nipple when Genevieve's hand snaked between her legs again.

Ah, fuck, that was too much. Mia did the same, reaching for Genevieve's clit, swiping up from her pussy to get it nice and wet.

For a few moments, there was no sound except

their labored breathing. Genevieve's fingers felt like sweet heaven, and judging by the desperate little whimpers Genevieve was making, she was as close to coming as Mia was.

"Same time," Mia gasped. "Tell me when."

She was ready to come at a moment's notice, her legs tensed and her mind desperately scrambling for control. She wanted to fall over the edge with Genevieve, but she wasn't sure how much longer she could hold out.

Fortunately, she didn't have to do so for long. Less than ten seconds later, Genevieve stiffened beneath her. "Now, Mia! Fuck, I'm coming now!"

Mia let go. She pressed herself closer to Genevieve as she shuddered through her orgasm, her hand cramping on Genevieve's clit, but she didn't let up. Genevieve was coming too, crying out Mia's name, and it was the hottest thing Mia had ever heard.

The orgasm faded slowly. Genevieve removed her hand just as it started to become too much, and Mia did the same with her.

Mia realized that they had somehow rolled off the beanbag onto the floor. In the heat of passion, she hadn't noticed. The floor was hard, cold and not particularly inviting. Mia felt too good to move, though, so she would have to settle for the floor.

Apparently, Genevieve felt differently. "Mia. Let's move this back to the beanbag."

"Mhmm." Mia made no effort to move. Genevieve chuckled and grabbed her under the arms, hauling her into the center of the beanbag.

Mia squeaked in indignation, but she was too pleased with the way they ended up tangled together in the dent in the beanbag's center to protest much.

It felt so good here. She had cuddled after sex before, of course, but it had never felt like this. Mia felt like she could do this forever.

Mia felt her eyes drifting shut. It probably wasn't a good idea to fall asleep with Genevieve— her new boss—like this, but she found she didn't really care right now.

She listened to comforting sound of Genevieve's heartbeat as she drifted off.

Mia woke stiff and confused. The light, which had been fading when she had fallen asleep, was now brighter and coming from a completely different direction.

Fuck, what time was it?

She was entangled in Genevieve's arms.

Genevieve was still deeply asleep, and Mia didn't want to wake her. She stared hopelessly at her purse, which had her phone in it and was clear on the other side of the room.

Mia glanced at the window again and tried to judge the time from the quality and angle of the light. Oh, who was she kidding? She wasn't some character in a novel from a time when they didn't have cell phones for such things. She had no idea. However, the fact that there was light at all made it clear that it was sometime after sunrise.

Mia's eyes widened as the true implications of that sunk in. She had slept the entire night here with Genevieve.

She had slept *without nightmares.*

That hardly ever happened. Maybe a couple of times a year. Was it a coincidence, or was it something to do with Genevieve? Mia remembered how safe and content she had felt falling asleep in Genevieve's arms. It wouldn't surprise her if that had something to do with it.

Mia would have to digest all that later. For now, she needed to think about more urgent issues— like what to do when Genevieve woke up.

Had Genevieve meant to fall asleep with her, or

had it been a mistake on her part as well? How would she react when she woke up?

The last thing Mia wanted was to lose the once-in-a-lifetime career opportunity Genevieve was offering her. She didn't know how Genevieve would feel waking up like this. What if it messed things up between them professionally?

Before Mia could go too far down that line of thought, Genevieve stirred. Mia felt her heartrate ratchet up. What was she going to do? Act cool and brush it off? Try to talk about it?

It was too late to come up with strategies now. Genevieve's eyes fluttered open.

"Oh." Her brow wrinkled adorably in confusion as she looked at Mia. "I guess we fell asleep."

She didn't seem upset, and the knot in Mia's stomach loosened slightly. "Yeah. Sorry about that."

Genevieve shrugged. "It's understandable. Yesterday was... intense." She grinned at Mia. "I've never had anything like that, to be honest."

"Me neither," Mia admitted. Her stomach rumbled. "Do you want some breakfast?"

"Sure."

Mia was encouraged by how casually

Genevieve was taking this. Perhaps all her panic earlier had been for nothing.

Genevieve followed her to the kitchen, and Mia started getting out stuff for French toast. She didn't usually put this much effort into her breakfast, but she wanted to do something nice for Genevieve.

"So, how did you sleep?"

Mia hesitated but decided to be honest. "Really well, actually. Better than I've slept in a long time. I... I didn't have any nightmares."

"That's great. Does that not happen often?"

"No, not often at all. It might have been a coincidence, but maybe not."

"Well, we should try it again sometime."

Mia ran these words through her head several times to be sure she was understanding right. "You mean the sleeping together, or...?" She trailed off. She couldn't deny that the idea of being with Genevieve more—both for sex and for sleeping in each other's arms—was enticing.

"Either. Both. Whatever you'd like."

"Both," Mia said at once. No way was she turning down an opportunity to get more nights without nightmares—and with steamy sex in the bargain? She'd be crazy to say no.

"Both, then," Genevieve agreed.

Mia's heart seemed to expand a little in her chest. She had a good feeling about this.

5

GENEVIEVE

Genevieve had never meant to fall asleep with Mia, but she wasn't exactly unhappy about it. More... antsy.

She liked the idea of taking this further with Mia, but she was also hesitant. Like Kate, Mia had past trauma, and Genevieve's experiences with women who had past trauma were far from pleasant.

"Are you okay?"

Genevieve startled out of her thoughts. She hadn't realized that Mia could read her expressions so easily.

"Just thinking..."

"Care to share?"

Genevieve considered for a moment. "I'll trade you? My sad past for yours?"

Mia's eyes became faraway for a moment, but when she focused on Genevieve again, she seemed determined. "Alright. I... I haven't really talked to anyone about this before, but maybe it's time that I do."

"You don't have to if you don't want to."

"I know... but I feel comfortable with you." Mia took a deep breath. "My stepfather was... well, he was a lot of things, but an alcoholic was one of them. He was a mean drunk. He never touched me, but he would shout a lot and throw things at the walls. One day when I was twelve, I brought home a sculpture I'd made in art class. I was really proud of it. He got angry when I tried to show it to him and smashed it against the table."

"I'm so sorry, Mia. No one deserves that kind of treatment, least of all a child."

"Yeah. I still get nightmares about it most nights. I know it's stupid. There are plenty of people who were in worse situations than me and handled it better. And he was awful to my mum."

"It's not stupid. Abuse is abuse. Whether or not he touched you, your trauma is just as valid as anyone else's. And having to watch your mum go through what she did... well, that must have been so tough for you."

"Yeah, I just wanted to protect her so much. But I couldn't do anything. It was so hard."

Genevieve had known that Mia had something in her past but being let in on the secret didn't do much to dispel her worry.

"What about you?"

"I had a girlfriend before—a while ago now. Her name was Kate. She also had a traumatic past. I won't get into details—that's not for me to tell—but her past caught up with her. I thought she loved me enough to stay, to let me help her work things out. She didn't. She ran away. One day, she was there, and the next, she had moved cities and changed her number. I never heard from her again."

"Wow. I'm so sorry that happened to you, Genevieve. You deserve better than that."

Genevieve shrugged. "After that... well, I'm hesitant to get involved with anyone else."

"I can understand that. Anyone would be hesitant under those circumstances. I'm not her, though, Genevieve. I won't run."

Genevieve quickly backtracked. "It's not the same. I mean, it's not like we're in a relationship.

Sleeping together is something entirely different to what Kate and I had."

"It doesn't have to be. You deserve a real relationship, with someone who won't betray you. I mean, if it's something you want."

"I don't miss Kate, not anymore, but I miss what we had. I miss the companionship, the knowledge that I was someone's everything, just as she was mine. But I'm not risking my heart like that again."

"Where will you get in life without some risk? You're a CEO, you should know that. Would you have built up a successful business without taking risks?"

"No," Genevieve admitted. "It's not the same thing, though."

"No, it's not. The stakes are higher, but so are the rewards. Let's try, Genevieve. I want more than sex and dreamless nights from you. I want all of you. We have a connection; I know you can feel it too. I really think we can make this work."

Genevieve was torn. Mia's lovely green eyes were earnest and sparkling. She could see what Mia was offering, and she wanted it. Wanted it bad. She hadn't felt like this for anyone since Kate, and if she turned Mia down, she might be missing an opportunity that would never come again.

But if she took Mia up on her offer, she would be opening herself up to history repeating itself.

"I don't know, Mia. It's... I haven't had any kind of personal relationship in years. I don't know if I can do it."

"We can figure it out together. I'm not worried about that. I'm not going to expect you not to make mistakes, or not to get scared. But if you don't want this, I won't try to push it on you."

"It's not that I don't want it. I just... I guess I'm just scared. I don't really know which course of action is best."

"Well, I can't make that decision for you. But I want you to know that if you're in, I'm in as well."

Maybe this was a bad idea, but Mia was filling Genevieve with confidence and hope for the future.

"I think I want to try. We'll need to go slow—at least on the dating part. I'm certainly not walking things back as far as the sex is concerned."

"You'll have no arguments from me there. I don't want this to affect our professional relationship, though. I think we'll make a good team, both inside and outside the office, but if one doesn't work out…"

"We won't let it affect us," Genevieve promised. "That's something I can guarantee. I always put my business first, and no matter what happens between us personally, you're a good investment. I'm certainly not going to let go of you if I have any choice in the matter."

"Then I guess we have a deal. There's just one more thing to arrange."

"Oh yeah? What's that?"

"Where do you want to go on our first date?"

Genevieve didn't remember the last time she felt so excited about arranging anything.

6

MIA

Mia hadn't been this nervous for a date in a long while. She hadn't liked anyone as much as she liked Genevieve... well, ever. She looked at herself in the mirror, reminding herself that Genevieve was already attracted to her and that wasn't going to change based on whether she wore the red halter neck or the navy blue cocktail dress.

Genevieve hadn't told her where they were going, but she had told Mia to dress fancy, which limited her choices. Genevieve probably had a whole wardrobe of fancy evening clothes, but Mia seldom went to such events, and had only these two choices.

She eventually decided to go with the red—who didn't look good in red?

Genevieve was picking her up, wanting to keep the location a surprise.

Mia was just starting with her makeup when the doorbell rang. She glanced at her watch in panic. It was still quarter to seven. She had fifteen minutes left to get ready—or so she had thought.

She dashed to the door, her lipstick still clutched in her hand, and pulled it open.

There was Genevieve, holding a bunch of red roses that were a near-perfect match for Mia's dress.

"Oh," Mia said stupidly. "You're early."

"Sorry—I guess I was a bit over-eager. I can wait in the car if you're not ready for me?"

"No, please, come inside. I just need to finish my makeup, and then we can go."

"I'll put these in water. You go do your thing."

As frazzled as she had been when she opened the door, Genevieve's easy manner quickly put Mia at ease.

She went back to her room and put on her makeup, trying not to hurry too much to avoid making mistakes. When she was done, she found Genevieve putting the flowers in vase for her.

Mia wanted to kiss her, but she was afraid of getting her bright red lipstick on Genevieve's lips, which looked utterly luscious in a pale pink lip gloss that matched her light pink dress perfectly.

"You look beautiful."

"So do you. I'd kiss you, but I don't think red lipstick would look very good with this dress."

Mia chuckled. "I was just thinking the same thing."

She loved how she and Genevieve always seemed to be on the same wavelength. Instead of kissing her, Mia leaned in and pulled Genevieve into a hug. They stayed there for several moments, enjoying the simple feeling of being in each other's arms.

"Shall we go?" Genevieve asked after a minute.

"Yeah, let's go."

Genevieve drove for twenty minutes, slightly out of the main bustle of the city, to a fancy Italian place with fairy lights wrapped around the trees in their expansive garden.

"This place is beautiful. How did you find it?"

"A client introduced me to it. He spent the whole night hitting on me. I only told him after he'd signed the contract that I'm gay."

Mia snorted. "I bet he wasn't impressed."

"No, not particularly. He got over it once he started seeing results from our partnership, though. If there's one thing men like more than sex, it's money."

"You have that right."

One of the waiters took them inside. Mia felt self-conscious in her fancy dress and couldn't help eyeing the other customers, comparing herself to them and wondering if she was dressed right.

Genevieve seemed to read her mind. "You look beautiful—like you belong here."

"How do you do that?"

"Do what?"

"Know what I'm thinking."

Genevieve shrugged. "Maybe I'm psychic and using my witchly powers on you."

"Oh yeah? I'd like to see what else those witchly powers can do. Do they extend past public spaces?"

Genevieve smirked. "I guess you'll find out soon enough."

They ordered and chatted as they waited for the food to arrive. Mia had been worried that things would be awkward—first date and all—but she and Genevieve connected easily and never struggled for things to talk about.

"Have you given any more thought to the series you'll be working on?"

"I was actually working on the proposal today. I should have it ready for you by tomorrow."

"Care to give me an advanced peek?"

"Well, the idea I have isn't my usual work. If you'd like something more according to my typical style, I can always modify, but... well, I was thinking about doing a series of women. I'll sketch out some of my ideas, but it'll be things like a naked woman lying over rocks near a waterfall or in a field of flowers. I can always cover anything important if the nudity is going to be an issue."

"You do whatever you think will be best for your brand, and I'll promote it. I'm all for body positivity, and nudity isn't going to be an issue for me."

Yeah, Mia was definitely going to like working with Genevieve.

"There's one other thing. A request, one you're welcome to say no to."

"Well now I'm intrigued."

"I'd like you to model for me," Mia blurted out.

"Model? As in, for your paintings?"

"Obviously I wouldn't make them look exactly like you, but you inspire me. I know some places we could go where we wouldn't be disturbed, or where we could book out the venue. I mean, lying naked on the ground or on rocks certainly isn't for everyone, and I could always hire a model... but you're the one who inspired this idea in the first place. I'd love it if it could be you."

"I inspired you?"

"You have to know what you look like, Genevieve. I love the curves of your body, the lovely smoothness of your skin. I love the effortless grace that you exude whenever you move. You embody beauty."

Genevieve blushed and Mia enjoyed that she had caught her off guard for once. "If you think it'll help with your work, I'll gladly model for you."

"Perfect. Shall we make that our next date?" Mia was already running through options in her head. She knew of a sunflower farm nearby. Or would it look better in a field of lavender? She concluded that Genevieve—especially a naked Genevieve—would look good anywhere, but the sunflowers might go better with her skin tone.

"That sounds great. Where do you want to go?"

"Oh no, you don't get to know that yet. You got to keep this date a secret until the last moment. Now, it's time for me to return the favor."

"I hate surprises," Genevieve grumbled.

"Trust me, you'll love this one."

"You know, there's a hiking route a few miles away that could be perfect for one of our modeling sessions. There's a small trail that not many people know about, leading to a lake. I remember one rock that was partially in the water, which was perfect to lie on. I bet I could swim to it without getting my hair wet. Then I could lie on it and you could paint me there?"

Mia was already imagining it. Sunlight glinting off Genevieve's wet body, with Genevieve's pale hair lifted slightly from a light breeze. The image was as beautiful as it was enticing.

"That can be our third date. I'd better get some new canvases. This is going to be great."

They discussed ideas for paintings for a while before moving onto other subjects. Mia was having such a good time talking to Genevieve that she barely noticed what she was eating. The food was pleasant, but not nearly as pleasant as the warmth of Genevieve's palm against hers when they held hands over the table.

The time slipped away from them, and all too soon, the manager was informing them that the restaurant was closing. Mia was surprised to see that it was nearly midnight and they were the last guests left.

"I guess we overstayed our welcome."

Genevieve shrugged. "They'll get over it. They know me here—I always tip well and never give them any trouble."

"So you come here often?"

"Yeah, I've taken to bringing clients here. I remember the last time—"

The manager cleared his throat.

"Oh, right. Leaving. Yes, here you go."

Genevieve handed over her card and stood up. Mia did the same and took Genevieve's hand again.

The two of them strolled through the garden on their way to the car. Mia wished they had time to explore further, but the manager was already giving them the stink eye as they took a circuitous route back to the parking lot, and she didn't want to push her luck.

As they got into the car, exhaustion hit Mia. She hadn't realized how tired she was, she'd been having so much fun with Genevieve.

She glanced at Genevieve, wondering what she was expecting when they got home. The idea of making sweet love until the sun came up was delicious, but Mia's eyes were already drooping and she didn't want to fall asleep on Genevieve halfway through what was meant to be a passionate encounter.

"Do you want to come inside?" Mia asked as Genevieve walked her to the door.

"I'd love to. I'm afraid I'm not up to much, though. It's been a long night—extremely pleasant, but long. I'd be delighted to sleep beside you, though, and maybe we could do more in the morning?"

Mia almost laughed. Of course she and Genevieve would be on the same page. They usually were.

"That sounds great. I'm also really tired."

Tired though she may be, that didn't stop Mia from watching Genevieve as she undressed. She wondered...

"If I'm awake first tomorrow, can I wake you up with oral sex?"

Genevieve dropped the dress she was currently folding up and turned to face Mia. "You want to do that?"

"Only if you want to."

"Fuck, yes. Though I don't know how I'm going to sleep now, knowing what's coming."

"Well, if you don't sleep, you can hardly wake up with me going down on you, now can you?"

"That is a very good point. I suppose we'd best get to bed, then."

Mia quietly set an alarm on her phone, wanting to be sure to be the first one to wake up. She was already looking forward to tomorrow, so much that she wasn't even worried about nightmares.

She cuddled up close to Genevieve and closed her eyes.

When she next opened them, it was to the soft buzzing of her alarm.

Huh. She'd done it again—not a single nightmare. This was probably more than a coincidence. It had to be Genevieve.

Mia quickly shut off the alarm and carefully extracted herself from Genevieve's arms. She pulled back the covers, watching Genevieve the whole time for signs of wakefulness. Fortunately, Genevieve seemed to be deeply asleep, not even stirring as Mia pushed her night shirt up her legs.

Genevieve's legs were too close together for Mia to fit her head between them, so she started by licking a finger to moisten it and pushing it between her thighs, sliding it up until she could feel Genevieve's clit. Mia rubbed lightly, not wanting to wake Genevieve just yet.

As Mia kept rubbing, Genevieve let out a long moan and rolled over, her legs spreading automatically. Mia glanced up at her face, but Genevieve's eyes were still closed, her breathing still deep and even. She was certainly still asleep, but not for long.

With space for her head to fit easily now, Mia started licking Genevieve's clit. The taste and feeling of Genevieve under her tongue set Mia alight, and she longed to do more, but she hadn't gotten consent for anything more, and she certainly wasn't going to get that consent while Genevieve was asleep, so she simply continued licking Genevieve with increasing enthusiasm. She was getting wetter and wetter and Mia thought she would never tire of the taste of her.

Genevieve's breathing hitched and her eyes fluttered open. "Oh. *Ooh,* yes, Mia. Fuck, that's... oh my god, yes."

She bent her knees and placed her feet on the mattress, giving Mia better access, thrusting her hips forward to meet Mia's tongue. Mia could see that Genevieve's eyes were still bleary with sleep.

Waking up like this had taken her off guard, but she certainly didn't seem unhappy about it.

Genevieve's head lolled back against the pillow as she panted, rolling her hips toward Mia. Mia's body was urgently clamoring for attention, but she ignored it for now, focusing on Genevieve, whose thighs were trembling as she approached her climax.

Mia experimented with different touches of her tongue, hitting gold when she started flicking Genevieve's clit with the tip of her tongue, quick and firm.

"I'm gonna come... Mia, if you keep doing that, I'm going to... going to—oh yes, fuck, Mia! YES!"

Genevieve's hips came completely off the mattress as she grabbed Mia's head, pressing her down more firmly onto her clit.

Mia flicked her tongue back and forth for all she was worth as Genevieve came hard, crying out and writhing beneath her. Mia stopped licking only once she was sure she had wrung every last ounce of pleasure out of Genevieve's orgasm.

She had barely finished pulling away before her hand was in her own panties, rubbing urgently on her clit.

"Let me do that."

"Yeah," Mia gasped, but made no move to remove her hand. It felt so good, she couldn't stop. Getting Genevieve off like that had been wildly erotic and had her right on the edge of coming.

Genevieve chuckled and flipped Mia over. Mia moaned, still not taking her hand off her swollen clit.

The next thing she knew, Genevieve was grabbing her wrist and moving it away. Before Mia could think to protest, Genevieve replaced Mia's hand with her own, and then she had nothing to protest about. Genevieve's hand was so much better than Mia's, and she found herself hurtling toward her release faster than ever.

Mia was hit by her orgasm so fast she didn't even have time to brace for it. It just came at her like a whirlwind, sweeping her away on a tide of pleasure. Genevieve's fingers seemed to reach right through her body, touching every sensitive nerve ending and setting them alight.

It ended slowly, fading into short bursts as Genevieve kept rubbing on her clit, drawing the orgasm out until the touch was almost agonizing.

Mia rolled away, pulling Genevieve with her so that they tumbled to the other side of the bed in each other's arms.

Mia leaned forward and kissed Genevieve. "Good morning."

Genevieve laughed. "That was the best good morning I've ever had."

"I'm glad you enjoyed it. Does that mean I'm free to repeat it?"

"Only if I can do the same for you."

Mia didn't have to consider this for long. "Let's do it. If nothing else, it'll chase away any bad dreams that are lingering in the morning."

"Did you have one last night?"

"Nope. Free and clear. It must be you and your witchly powers."

"I told you I could work magic."

"I don't know... I'm not quite convinced yet."

Genevieve gave her a wicked grin. "Then let me show you exactly how magical my tongue can be."

She pushed Mia flat onto her back and straddled her before leaning in for a kiss.

Mia had never thought she could feel like this. Before these last few weeks with Genevieve, she would have told anyone who asked that she had been in love before.

Now, Mia could only come to the conclusion that before Genevieve, she hadn't known what love truly was. She hadn't realized that she could feel so *much* for another person. It was somehow overwhelming and comforting at the same time.

Mia hadn't said the words yet, but she knew what was in her heart. Still, it was probably too soon for Genevieve. It had only been a few weeks, after all. She knew Genevieve cared for her, but she didn't know if it was love yet, and she didn't want to put Genevieve in the awkward position of not being able to say it back.

No, she was content to wait until she was sure she could receive the answer she was looking for.

They hadn't moved in together officially, but they spent almost every night together, either at Mia's place or Genevieve's.

Mia went to sleep as usual, wrapped up with Genevieve, their limbs entangled after making sweet love to each other.

She woke up with a start in the middle of the night, the images flashing before her eyes.

Mia saw her stepfather screaming at her mother while she cowered in a corner, trembling. Running to her room as glass smashed behind her.

Cowering in a corner watching him get progressively more and more drunk.

Mia gasped, trying to catch her breath, but there didn't seem to be enough oxygen in the room.

Pull yourself together, Mia. This wasn't the first time she'd woken up from a nightmare having a panic attack, and after weeks without nightmares, this one had caught her off guard.

Still, she should be able to deal with it.

Mia desperately tried to pull air into her lungs, but it felt like she was breathing pure carbon dioxide. She knew very well that hyperventilating would only make matters worse, but she couldn't seem to help it.

"Mia? Mia, what's wrong?"

Mia clutched at Genevieve's wrist, trying to get the words out. "Can't breathe," she finally gasped.

Genevieve sat up in bed. "Medical condition or panic attack?"

Mia couldn't answer; she was too busy trying to breathe.

"You can just shake or nod your head. Medical condition?"

Mia shook her head jerkily.

"Panic attack?"

Mia nodded as best she could.

"Okay." Genevieve took both of Mia's hands in hers. "Just breathe, sweetheart. All you need to do is slow down. I promise, you can breathe, but you're trying to go too fast. Slowly."

Mia tried, she really did, but the oxygen escaped her.

Genevieve let go of one of Mia's hands and turned the bedside lamp on. "Just follow my hand. Breathe in..."

She lifted her hand slowly in the air.

"Now breathe out."

Her hand went down again. Mia watched Genevieve's hand, trying to match her breaths to the slow movement. Genevieve's calm, assured manner helped to soothe her somewhat, to convince her that she wasn't actually dying, even if it felt like she was.

Mia took shuddering breaths, following Genevieve's hand. As she got herself more under control, Genevieve's movements got slower and slower, forcing Mia to breathe more slowly as well. Tears of relief filled Mia's eyes as she finally started to feel like she was getting the oxygen she needed.

Genevieve pulled her into a hug. "There go. I've got you, Mia."

For the first time in a long time, Mia allowed herself to let go with another person. She hugged Genevieve as she cried into her shoulder. Genevieve simply held her tighter, waiting for her to calm.

When she did, Mia pulled away, embarrassed. "I'm sorry. You've got an early morning tomorrow, and here I am disturbing your sleep."

Genevieve gave her an incredulous look. "You think I care about that? I care about *you*. Do you want to talk? What do you need?"

Mia shrugged. "It's nothing, really. Just a nightmare. I'm not used to them anymore, so I got caught off guard and didn't handle it very well."

"Do you often get panic attacks?"

"Not as often as I used to, but they turn up every now and then."

"Have you ever considered therapy?"

Mia grimaced. "Yeah, I have... but I'm not so keen on telling a stranger about... well, everything."

"I know it must be intimidating, but I really think it might be worth it. There are treatments for PTSD, and I think they could really help you."

"I do know that," Mia sighed. "Logically, it makes perfect sense. I guess I'm just scared."

"If you'd like, I could come to the appointment with you. It might be easier to talk to a stranger if you know you have a friendly face waiting in reception when you're done."

Mia had to admit that this idea did sound easier than trying to force herself to go on her own. "I'll consider that. Thank you."

"It's my pleasure. Whatever you need, Mia. I'm here for you."

"Thank you." Mia pulled Genevieve back down into bed and cuddled into her, her head laying on Genevieve's chest.

She was scared to sleep again, but the rhythmic sound of Genevieve's breathing soon had her dozing off.

This time, she slept without nightmares.

7

GENEVIEVE

Genevieve ambled to the lounge, glancing at her watch. It was five to six, and Mia was never late. Just a few minutes, and her stupidly long day would suddenly look a lot brighter.

Genevieve spent the time going over pleasant memories in her head. Just a few days ago, she and Mia had gone to a sunflower farm. Mia had taken her camera and snapped some shots of Genevieve —naked in various poses among the flowers— before sitting down to paint. Genevieve idly picked up her phone and started scrolling through the photos.

Once Mia had all the shots she'd wanted,

Genevieve had insisted on taking some of her, equally naked, just to be fair, of course. Fortunately, they'd had their clothes on by the time one of the gardeners came past, who had kindly obliged them by taking several photos of them together.

Genevieve smiled as she looked through pictures of her and Mia among the sunflowers. It had been a great date.

When she looked at the time again, she saw that it was ten past six. Genevieve frowned. Mia was never late.

She sent a quick text.

Hey, Mia, are we still on for tonight?

Genevieve waited a few minutes, but there was no response.

Mia, is everything ok?

Still nothing.

.   .   .

Please respond to this so that I know you're alright.

When there was no response to that, Genevieve
gave Mia a call. The phone rang and rang with no
answer. Now, Genevieve was truly concerned. She
called three more times before getting into her car.
Maybe Mia was at home. She might be sick or
hurt. Genevieve couldn't think of anything else
that would prevent Mia from at least telling her
that she couldn't make it.

Genevieve made it to Mia's house in record
time and rang the bell. Nothing.

She knocked on the door. "Mia? Mia, if you're
in there, say something, please. I'm really worried."

The house was as silent as a tomb.

Fuck. This wasn't good.

Genevieve tried not to panic as she drove to the
police station, but she couldn't stop her hands
from shaking. If something had happened to
Mia... Well, Genevieve didn't know what she'd do
without her.

Over the past few months, Mia had become
central to her life. Genevieve's work still fulfilled

her, but there was nothing like coming home after a long day to Mia's sweet smile and the floral scent of her perfume as she put her arms around Genevieve and asked how her day was.

There was no one immediately available at the station, so Genevieve grabbed the arm of a busy-looking officer walking past.

"Please, I need help. I think something has happened to my girlfriend."

His expression immediately became serious. "Let's sit over here. Tell me what happened."

Genevieve allowed herself to be ushered into a chair, trying to remain calm. "She was supposed to meet me tonight at my place. She's never late and she hardly ever cancels. When she does, she always lets me know at least a few hours before-hand. Tonight, she just never showed up. I called her and even went to her house, but there's no one there."

"When was the last time you spoke to her?"

"This morning. I was at her place last night and we had breakfast together before I headed off to work. She was going to spend the day at home, working on her paintings. I don't know what could have happened. She could be sick or hurt or kidnapped—"

"Let's try not to think the worst. Ninety percent of the time, these kinds of disappearances are nothing sinister. She may have simply forgotten her phone at home and gone out."

"She wouldn't forget that we had plans. She never forgets."

"Everyone forgets sometimes. No one is perfect."

"I'm not saying everyone is perfect," Genevieve snapped. "I'm saying I know her. She wouldn't forget."

"I understand. I'll have one of the officers check on her."

"Can I come with? Please?"

"Absolutely not. We don't allow civilians in the field. Don't worry, they'll call as soon as they know anything."

Genevieve paced up and down the station, jumping every time the phone rang. Officer Williams, who was helping her, answered calmly each time, and each time, he shook his head at Genevieve. No news on Mia yet.

Another call came, and this time, Officer Williams sat up straighter. He beckoned Genevieve forward. Genevieve nearly tripped over her own feet in her hurry to get to him.

"I see. Uh-huh. Yeah. Okay, thanks, Bryan. I'll tell her."

He hung up. Genevieve's fingernails were digging painfully into her palms. "What happened? Where is she?"

"You can stop worrying, Genevieve. Mia is perfectly fine."

"Fine? What do you mean? Where is she?"

"I'm afraid I'm not at liberty to say. What I can tell you is that she's safe, and she has her phone with her. If she wants to contact you, she will."

"That makes no sense. Why would she be somewhere else when she was supposed to meet me? Why would she not answer her phone if she's not in some kind of trouble?"

"All I can say is that my colleagues have checked on her personally and assure me that she is fine. I can't go interfering in relationship issues when no one is in danger."

Genevieve wanted to scream and shake the answers out of him, but she still retained enough of her sanity to know that this would be a very bad idea.

"Please, could you have them ask her to call me?"

"They have already told her that you're trying to get in touch. I'm afraid that's all we can do."

Genevieve stared dumbly at him. She felt like she might be going into shock. Mia didn't want to talk to her?

That made no sense. Mia always came to Genevieve with her problems, just as Genevieve did with Mia. What could have happened to make it otherwise?

Genevieve sank heavily into a chair as memories of Kate bombarded her. This was exactly how things had ended with Kate. Just... nothing. No calls, no explanation, no contact.

Was history repeating itself?

A couple of hours ago, Genevieve would have said that was impossible, that Mia would never do that to her, but what was she supposed to think now? Officer Williams had confirmed that Mia was safe and free to contact her if she wanted to.

Had Genevieve done something? She frantically wracked her brain, going over their last couple of interactions. Mia hadn't been acting oddly at all. Everything between them had been great, at least from Genevieve's point of view.

She went home, half-expecting to see Mia on

her doorstep with a bunch of flowers and an apology, but her driveway was depressingly empty.

Genevieve wandered inside, moving aimlessly from room to room. She didn't know what to do. What did she do with her evenings before Mia? She could barely even remember a time before Mia.

Eventually, she decided to get an early night. Surely, Mia would contact her tomorrow.

Mia didn't contact her the next day, or the one after, or even the one after that.

A week passed with complete radio silence. Genevieve's initial dismay started curdling into hot anger. She hadn't done anything wrong. She didn't deserve to be treated this way. If Mia didn't want to be with her anymore, then she at least owed Genevieve the decency of telling her so.

She had been right all along. Getting involved with Mia was a mistake. It was said that you attracted the same kinds of people in relationships. Well, Genevieve should have listened to that theory sooner. Not only did she seem to attract people who would leave, but people who would leave her without a word or any form of closure.

This was never going to happen again. Genevieve had been an idiot for letting Mia worm her way into her heart. She was just busy berating herself for exactly how stupid she had been when the doorbell rang.

Genevieve was still lost in her disgruntled thoughts as she opened it, expecting a delivery, and it took a moment for her to register what she was seeing.

Mia was there, standing right in front of her.

Genevieve swayed on her feet as she was bombarded by conflicting emotions. She didn't know whether she wanted to scream at Mia or kiss her.

In the end, she did neither. Genevieve folded her arms tightly across her chest. "What are you doing here, Mia?"

"Please, Genevieve, can we talk?"

"If you wanted to talk to me, you should have done so a week ago. I've been worried sick about you. Did you know I went to the police? I thought you'd been kidnapped!"

Mia hung her head. "I know. I'm so sorry, Genevieve. I understand if you can't forgive me, but please, could you at least allow me the opportunity to explain?"

Genevieve was sorely tempted to slam the door in Mia's face, but Mia looked so distraught that she couldn't bring herself to do it. Her dark hair was up in a messy bun, her big green eyes looked like they had been crying.

"Fine."

Mia had better have a fucking good explanation for this, or Genevieve was going to revisit the kicking her out and slamming the door in her face idea.

Mia fiddled with her hands as she sat on the couch opposite Genevieve. "I told you about my stepfather, but I never really talked much about my mother."

This wasn't the direction she had expected the conversation to go in. "That's right," Genevieve said guardedly. "What of it?"

"Well, my mother was never abusive, but she sat by and let the abuse happen to and around her, which is almost as bad when there's a child suffering that abuse with you. I begged her to get rid Harold, but she insisted that he would change his ways, that he was trying. I resent her almost as much as I do him for what I went through."

"That makes sense. She was your mother. She should have protected you."

"Harold died last week," Mia said quietly. "The first thing my mother did was get on a plane and come to find me. I never even knew that she knew where I was, but apparently, she found me through my work. Anyway, she came to tell me about Harold, as if him dying would make everything okay and we could pick up back where we left off."

Mia's face twisted in anger. "I told her to fuck off, but she won't leave me be. She's selfish and she doesn't want to be alone. She's rented a house in the city and she keeps hounding me, trying to convince me that I'm the selfish one and that my childhood wasn't nearly as bad as I make it out to be."

Genevieve felt an entirely new type of anger flare in her gut. "So get a restraining order. I know some good lawyers, I can refer you."

"It's no good. I've already spoken to a lawyer, but since she's made no threat on my life, there isn't anything the police will be able to do at this point. I just need to stick it out. She'll get bored eventually. She doesn't handle rejection well, and when it becomes apparent that she's not going to get what she wants out of me, she'll move on— probably to the first abusive jerk who'll take her."

"Mia... I'm so sorry." Genevieve felt like a real jerk for having the thoughts she'd been having about Mia. She should have known better. She should have known that Mia wouldn't disappear like she had unless she was dealing with something really awful. "You should have spoken to me. I could have helped."

"Genevieve... please don't be angry, but... I think this is something I need to deal with myself. I don't want to drag you into this. I've booked an appointment with a therapist for next week. I'm going to try to work through my trauma and deal with this situation with my mom. I don't feel like I can fairly do that while maintaining a relationship. I don't want you to become my carer. I don't think that is fair on you and it isn't how I want things to be... I... I have to end things between us." Mia was crying now. Big tears running down her beautiful face.

Genevieve felt like she'd been hit in the chest with a block of ice. She had already suspected that her relationship with Mia was over, but to hear it stated so plainly was shattering.

She wanted to beg Mia to rethink, to stay, but she respected her too much to do that. Genevieve wanted Mia to do what was best for her and would never try to convince her to put anyone else's well-being above her own.

"Are you sure this is what you want, Mia?"

"I'm sure that it's what I *need* to do."

Genevieve held back her tears. There was no reason to make this any harder for Mia than it needed to be. If she begged for Mia to stay with her, maybe Mia would, but Genevieve would never ask Mia to do that when it wasn't what she needed.

"I understand, Mia. I wish you would stay, but if you feel you can't, I'll support you, and I'll be here. I'll wait for you. Whenever you're ready... I'm here."

Mia was already shaking her head. "Please, don't do that. I'm not sure if or when I'll be ready for a relationship. I don't want you to put your life on hold for me."

You are my life. I don't want anyone except you.

But Genevieve couldn't say that. This was hard enough for Mia as it was.

"Alright, Mia. I hear you."

She certainly wasn't going to promise not to move on with her life, but she didn't need to spell out exactly how crippled she would be without Mia.

Mia blinked a few times, tears escaping from the corners of her eyes. "I guess I should go, then."

I love you.

Genevieve battled to keep those words trapped

behind her lips. They wouldn't help and would only cause more hurt to both of them.

She wanted to ask Mia to stay just a little longer—she wasn't ready to say goodbye yet. But that would only get more and more difficult the longer Mia stayed, so Genevieve got up and walked robotically to the door. Mia followed her in silence.

It felt so wrong. Genevieve watched as Mia walked past her. Neither of them touched. Genevieve had never had many nightmares, but she certainly felt like she was in one now.

"Goodbye, Genevieve."

No, she wasn't ready. She would never be ready to say goodbye to Mia.

"Goodbye, Mia." Genevieve lost her battle to tears just as Mia turned away. She quickly closed her door and pressed her back to it, letting herself slide down to the floor.

She felt like she was in a nightmare, and she didn't know how to wake up.

"Maybe if we can just do this quickly enough, I can get back to Genevieve before she moves on."

Patrick raised an eyebrow. "Therapy can't be rushed, Mia."

"I'm a quick learner. Just tell me what to do."

"You need to calm down and stop expecting your problems to be solved in a few sessions. You've been carrying around this trauma since you were a child, and it's going to take time to unravel, especially with the complication of your mother being back in your life."

Mia resisted the urge to growl under her

breath. "I am not losing Genevieve because of my past or my mother."

"You seem determined to reestablish your relationship with her."

"Of course I am—I love her!"

"And yet, you told her not to wait for you."

"Damn right I did! It wouldn't be fair for me to ask her to put her life on hold because of my mental nonsense."

"The way you described it, it sounded like she was offering rather than you asking."

Mia clutched the sides of the seat to prevent herself from getting up and storming off. She had been embarrassed enough afterward the first time she did it. She did not need a rerun of that, or the questions that followed when she came back.

"Tell me what you're feeling."

"I'm feeling fucking annoyed, that's what! Do you really have to take everything and throw it back at me?"

"Do you feel I'm being unfair?"

Mia didn't have an answer to that question—at least not one she could put into words—so she settled for glaring at the corner of the desk.

"Are you sure this is really about being fair to

Genevieve? Do you not think you're afraid of being betrayed by someone close to you again?"

"I'm not afraid of Genevieve betraying me. She would never do that."

"On a conscious level, I'm sure you're right, but what about the unconscious? Your mom was supposed to protect you, and she abandoned you —maybe not in the literal sense, but she wasn't there for you. That kind of thing doesn't come without its own scars. Do you think you might be scared to commit to Genevieve because you worry your issues will cause her to abandon you too?"

"No," Mia said stubbornly.

Patrick went quiet, leaving Mia with nothing but her thoughts. She hated when he did this. Now she had nothing to do except examine what he had said and see if there was any truth to it—and unfortunately, there did seem to be a fair amount of truth in there.

"Fine, maybe you're right," she grumbled after a few minutes of silence. "I don't see how knowing that helps me, though. Aren't you supposed to be able to work some magic to fix my brain?"

"Only you can fix your brain, Mia. I'm simply here to guide you along the process."

"If I'm the only one who can fix my brain, then

I'm fucking doomed, aren't I?" Mia was usually politer than this, but therapy worked on her last nerve and she couldn't help snapping. Fortunately, Patrick was unflappably calm and didn't seem to take offense easily.

"Why are you still here, Mia? I can see you don't like me. It's been four sessions. What keeps you coming back?"

"It's not that I don't like you," Mia said grudgingly. She actually really did like Patrick and thought in other circumstances that they could even have been friends. "It's the therapy. I don't like people poking around in my head."

"It makes you feel afraid? Vulnerable?"

"I guess. But I need to do this—for Genevieve, and myself."

"I'm glad you put yourself on that list, because therapy seldom works if you are doing it purely for another person."

"So when is it supposed to start working?"

"You tell me. Do you feel you've made any progress in the time you've been seeing me?"

Mia forced herself to think about it rather than giving an irritable, dismissive response.

"Honestly, I think things have only gotten worse. Not that I'm blaming you for that—and maybe they would have been even worse than they are now without you—but the longer I'm away from Genevieve, the worse it is. I feel like she was the last breath I took, and every day I'm apart from her, the more and more oxygen deprived I become."

"That doesn't sound particularly healthy. Couples should be able to function apart, no matter how close they are."

"Well, if I was healthy, I wouldn't be here now, would I?"

"I suppose not," Patrick conceded. "Tell me more about your mother. Have you heard anything else from her?"

"Not in the last week. Getting the neighborhood watch involved was a good idea. I've seen from the messages in the group that she's been chased off a few times by their patrols, but I don't imagine that'll deter her for long."

"You can't control her actions; you can only control yours. What do you think you'll do when you next come into contact with her?"

"Well, telling her to go to hell clearly hasn't had any effect. I was thinking of threatening legal action if she keeps harassing me. I know the police won't do anything to help, but *she* doesn't necessarily know that. Maybe if I hit her with an official letter from a lawyer, it'll scare her away."

"Do you think that'll work?"

Mia sighed. "Probably not."

"What do you think will work?"

"If I knew that, don't you think I'd do that?"

"Have you considered talking to her?"

"This entire exercise is so that I *don't* have to talk to her."

"I know that you don't want to pick up a relationship with her again, and I agree with you on that. I just think that perhaps if you talked to her, it might help. She clearly doesn't realize how badly she fucked up with you. Maybe if you explained it to her, she'd understand just how far past saving your relationship really is."

It wasn't a bad idea, but Mia didn't like it. She didn't want to bring up the past with her mom. That would surely only make things worse... but what if it was the only way to dissuade her?

"I'll think about it."

"You do that. Our time is up, but I'll see you next week."

"Thanks, Patrick," Mia said grudgingly. She left the office, grateful as she always was to be out from under Patrick's scrutiny.

It had been four weeks since she saw Genevieve, and the hole Genevieve had left inside her was as large and painful as ever. It was like the best parts of Mia had been ripped out, and she had no idea how to get them back. She wished she could see Genevieve's lovely blue eyes again. She missed them. She missed losing herself in Genevieve's kindness and the safety that she felt when she was with her.

The nightmares were worse than ever, and she was even having trouble with her art. That, more than anything, bothered her. Art had always been her solace, but it seemed like the passion she had for it had gone out of it. Mia had had plenty of passion for her work before she even met Genevieve but trying to convince herself that this passion should have remained untouched after Genevieve left was not having the desired results.

Mia went to bed wondering about the potential conversation with her mom. What would she say? She would have to give evidence, because her mom would surely argue against the charges. There was so much evidence, Mia didn't even know where to start.

Later, she understood that it had been a mistake to go to sleep pondering the worst things her stepfather had ever done, but that knowledge came too late to save her.

Mia shot up in bed, screaming her lungs out after one of the worst nightmares she'd ever had. Sobbing hysterically, she reached for her phone automatically, navigating to Genevieve's number with shaking fingers.

The phone rang for so long that Mia started to fear it wouldn't be picked up, but eventually, it was.

"Mia?"

"Gen-vieve—help—I—Gen—" Mia couldn't draw in enough breath to speak, nor do so clearly through her sobs. The world was spinning, and the thundering of her heart seemed to drown out all other noises.

"... are you? Mia, can you hear me? Where are you? Do you need an ambulance?"

"N-n-n—"

"Where are you?"

Mia managed to choke out the word *home* before falling back on the bed, clutching her chest as it sent sharp pains through her torso. She wondered if she'd been wrong in telling Genevieve she didn't need an ambulance, but how was she supposed to say that when she could barely muster enough oxygen to keep herself conscious?

"I'm on my way to you, Mia. Just hang in there. I'll be with you in ten minutes."

Ten minutes? How the hell was she supposed to survive like this for ten minutes? Mia spluttered incoherently but couldn't get words to come.

"I've got to hang up now to drive, but I'll see you soon. I've still got the spare key; I'll let myself in. You've got this, Mia."

The line clicked dead.

You've got this? Who was Genevieve kidding. Mia had never had anything less in her entire life.

She thrashed on the bed, desperately trying to breathe, her vision flashing between now and scenes from many years ago.

She was just trying to find her phone, which had dropped somewhere on the bed, to call 911, sure she was dying, when the door burst open.

"I'm here, I'm here." Genevieve gathered Mia into her arms, holding Mia's head to her chest. "I've got you, Mia. You're having a panic attack. Just breathe for me."

Mia drew in what felt like her first full breath in weeks. Just being held by Genevieve seemed to ease some of the constriction in her chest. She knew that Genevieve had helped Kate through many panic attacks, and she had refined those skills with Mia.

Mia clutched at Genevieve's shoulders for dear life, shaking and doing her best to breathe.

"Follow my hand, sweetheart. In... and out... in... and out..."

Mia lost herself in the familiar ritual. Genevieve didn't stop until her breathing was slow and even, though tears still ran thickly down her face.

Only now that she was calmer did Mia realize what she'd done. She had left Genevieve to protect her from this kind of mental nonsense, and now Mia had gone and drawn her right back into it.

She opened her mouth to apologize, but those weren't the words that came out. "Stay with me? Just for tonight? Please?"

"Of course, I'm not going anywhere. Come on, let's get you cleaned up." Genevieve went briefly to the bathroom and returned with a damp cloth that she used to tenderly wipe Mia's face. Mia had to admit that she felt better afterward. The idea of sleep wasn't exactly inviting, but she was exhausted by the ordeal, and when Genevieve coaxed her to lie down again, Mia didn't resist.

It took a long time for her to drift off again, but

eventually, Genevieve's steady heartbeat and breathing lulled her back to sleep.

When Mia woke, it didn't take long for the reality of the previous night to come crashing back to her. She could hardly deny that reality when she had one of her legs thrown over Genevieve's thigh and her arm trapped under Genevieve's waist.

Mia squeezed her eyes shut, wishing she could go back to the previous night and make better life choices.

Her choices had only hurt her more, because she now understood something she hadn't before.

She had been a fool to let Genevieve go. Genevieve had been willing to walk through this with her, and Mia should have let her. Genevieve was the love of her life, and Mia had thrown that love away.

But it was too late to do anything about that now. Mia loved Genevieve too much to mess around with her again. She knew that if she asked Genevieve to take her back, Genevieve would, which was exactly why Mia couldn't ask.

She was too unstable to maintain a steady relationship—last night showed that much. If she started again with Genevieve now, she would only hurt her. Genevieve would do everything she could to take care of Mia, and Mia would let her, to Genevieve's detriment.

Mia knew Genevieve's history. She wouldn't let that history repeat itself, not when she had any say in the matter.

"Genevieve. Genevieve, wake up."

"Mmm?"

Genevieve's eyes opened, slowly focusing on Mia. "Good morning. How are you feeling?"

Mia steeled herself. "You have to go."

Genevieve's air of sleepy contentment vanished as she stiffened. "What?"

"You have to go. This was a mistake."

"How can you say that? After last night... I thought you wanted me."

I do want you. More than you can possibly imagine.

Mia couldn't say that, though. She couldn't allow Genevieve to think there was hope for them. A clean break would be better.

"I was in a panic. I reacted badly. I'm sorry I pulled you into this. I wish I could take it back, but the best I can do now is try to correct that mistake. Please, I need you to go."

Mia hated the hurt on Genevieve's face, but she

knew that this was the least painful option, for Genevieve if not for herself.

"Mia, think about this. You know we're right together. We can do this. We can figure out a way through it together."

Mia braced herself for the biggest lie she'd ever told. "That's not what I want. I want you to go."

Genevieve stiffened. "If that's what you really want."

"It is."

"Then I suppose there's nothing more to say."

"No, there isn't," Mia whispered.

She watched Genevieve gather her clothes and leave, taking Mia's heart with her.

9

GENEVIEVE

enevieve couldn't believe this. She was torn between screaming in rage and melting into a puddle of despair on the ground.

She had thought that last night had been a turning point. When she'd comforted and held Mia last night, it had felt so right. She had been sure Mia had felt it too. Apparently, she had been wrong.

Perhaps it would be easier if she could focus on anger, but mostly, Genevieve felt hurt and heartbroken all over again. She had been there for Mia when Mia had really needed her, and her thanks was to be kicked out the next day like it was nothing. So much for hoping for a new start.

Maybe this whole thing with Mia was a mistake. Genevieve understood Mia's reasons for leaving initially, but now she just felt used. If Mia was the kind of person who could take advantage of someone like that, then perhaps she wasn't the person Genevieve had thought she was.

Well, she wasn't going to wait for Mia anymore. There would be no more staring at the phone, hoping Mia would call with the news that she was on the road to being healed and wanted to try again. Genevieve had already assigned someone else to work with Mia on their painting arrangement.

She had hoped that would be a temporary thing, but now, it would have to become permanent.

She would simply have to move on with her life, just like she had lived before Mia. How hard could that be?

"Genevieve, can we talk?"

"Of course. Come in, Penelope."

Penelope looked uncharacteristically nervous, which made Genevieve nervous in turn. She didn't particularly want to deal with any bad news in her business, not when things in her personal life were such a mess.

Penelope perched on the edge of one of the chairs in front of Genevieve's desk. "I need to talk to you."

"What is it?"

"I'm worried about you—we all are. The whole office."

This was not the direction Genevieve had expected the conversation to go in, and it most certainly wasn't a welcome surprise.

"I don't know what you're talking about," she said stiffly.

"Ever since you assigned Archer to work with Mia, we feel like things have gone downhill."

That made Genevieve sit up and pay attention. "You're unhappy? Is there trouble between Archer and Mia?"

This was something Genevieve could deal with. She frequently had to problem solve in her business, and if her employees were unhappy for some reason, she could tackle that problem head-on and solve it—unlike her personal problems, which were much less easily solvable.

"No, no, it's nothing like that. Archer and Mia work well together. None of us are unhappy, don't worry. We're just concerned for you—about *you* being unhappy."

Oh. Well, now they were back in territory Genevieve wanted nothing to do with.

"Thank you for your concern, Penelope, but please relay to everyone that I'm fine."

"I don't think you are. You've become more and more withdrawn ever since you and Mia split up. We were finally getting to know the real you, and now, we're losing you again."

"Maybe this is who I've always been. Perhaps I was just fighting to be someone I wasn't, and this is who I was always meant to be."

"Do you really believe that?"

"Yes," Genevieve lied through gritted teeth, trying to convince herself. "The thing with Mia was a mistake. I was better off before we ever met."

Genevieve half-expected Penelope to call bull-shit. She could tell that she wanted to. However, Genevieve was still Penelope's boss, and Penelope must have decided not to push this personal stuff.

"Alright, Genevieve. Just know that if you ever

want to talk, I'm available—so are most of the people here. We know you care about us—even if you don't say it—you show it to us in your actions, and we care about you too."

Genevieve's throat was suddenly unusually tight. She nodded and forced a smile. "Thank you, Penelope. I appreciate that."

Penelope hesitated, as though she had more to say, but thankfully, she seemed to think better of it. "I'll get back to work, then."

Genevieve nodded. She hadn't been doing as good of a job as she'd thought holding things together in front of others. Clearly, she needed to redouble her efforts.

Mia wasn't an option anymore. She had made sure to disabuse any notions Genevieve had of ever trying again. Genevieve would simply have to continue with her life, even if it felt like she was dying inside.

Her work still fulfilled her, as it always had, even before Mia. That was enough for her. It had to be enough.

10

MIA

"Hi, Mom."

"Mia, honey! It's so good to see you."

Mia gritted her teeth. It was just like her mom to pretend that nothing was wrong, and that none of the disastrous interactions in the past had even happened. But getting angry wouldn't help matters. That's not what she was here for.

"Please, sit down."

Mia pulled away slightly from her mom's open arms. She had agreed to meet her, but expecting a hug was pushing it too far.

Naomi either didn't notice or wasn't bothered. She had never cared to notice or be bothered by things that didn't fit into how she wanted the world to be.

"I've got us a nice little house, Mia, just on the other side of town. I've been trying to tell you about it, but... well, you're here now. We'll be together again, just like old times."

"Old times?" Old times like when Harry was harassing and terrifying the both of them? Mia once more had to clamp her mouth shut to stop herself from going on a tirade. She had a clear purpose here, and a tirade was not on the agenda.

"Mom, I asked you here for a reason. I have something I'd like to say, and I'd appreciate it if you could hear me out."

Mia knew the words of her speech by heart, having gone over it so many times that she could probably say it in her sleep.

"Of course. We're due for a good catch up."

Was she really that oblivious, or was she simply pretending nothing was wrong to lie to herself and assuage her own anxiety?

"Mom, Harry was abusive—toward both of us. He may not have hurt us physically, but it was still abuse."

"Mia, don't be silly. Harry would never have—"

"I asked you to hear me out. I promise I will

listen to what you have to say as well, but I would like to say my piece first."

"Okay, Mia. Whatever you want, honey."

"Like I said, Harry was abusive, and while you never joined him in that abuse, you did nothing to stop it. I was a child and couldn't do anything to protect myself. I was counting on you to protect me, and you didn't. I still have nightmares about it, you know. And panic attacks. What I went through has a far-reaching negative impact on me, something I will probably never be able to leave behind entirely." Mia took a deep breath and continued.

"You have hurt me too much for me to want you in my life again. What you did cannot be undone or explained away. I realize you may see it differently, but this is how I see it, and that's not going to change. I am asking you nicely to leave me alone. If you make me ask again, it will involve lawyers and it will not be nice."

"Mia, you're overreacting. Sure, Harry may have had a bit of a temper, but who doesn't have flaws? I'm your mother. You can't just end an entire relationship because of a little disagreement."

Mia really wanted to argue, but Patrick had told her not to do it. Arguing wouldn't bring her any sort of fulfillment and would only draw out this encounter.

"Is that everything you have to say?"

"I'm not on trial here, Mia."

"No, you're not. I've already made my decision. If you've said your piece, then there's nothing left to say."

"You can't just abandon your mother, Mia!"

"Like you abandoned your daughter? You may not have physically left, but you abandoned me all the same. I'm done. Stop contacting me or I will take legal action."

Mia had to get out of there before the desire to punch something overwhelmed her. It wasn't like her painting was going particularly well at the moment, but it would go even less well if she had a broken hand.

"Goodbye, Mom."

Naomi was staring at her, apparently shocked into silence. Mia was thankful that her mom didn't follow her as she left the restaurant.

By the time she got into the car, she was shaking hard, but she managed to hold it together until she got home. Her immediate instinct was to call Genevieve. She'd just done one of the hardest things she'd ever had to do, and she desperately needed reassurance. Genevieve would give her that, if Mia asked.

Despite everything that had passed between them, Mia knew that Genevieve would never turn her away when she was in distress.

However, she wasn't going to do that. It wouldn't be fair to Genevieve. Mia had already called Genevieve in crisis once, and it hadn't ended well. This time, she was going to do things properly.

She had finally gotten to the point of telling her mother goodbye for good. For the last several months, Mia had been working hard in therapy. She'd lost count of the number of times she'd wanted to strangle Patrick, but she couldn't deny that he'd been helpful.

It would probably take years to fully work through the trauma, but she felt like she was finally healed enough to offer Genevieve what she deserved—a stable partner who wasn't going to run out on her when things got hard.

Of course, Genevieve may not want that with Mia anymore, but Mia wasn't giving in without a fight. Genevieve had never had someone fight for her before. Mia was determined to be the first— and hopefully the last.

Mia went home and spent the afternoon using various self-soothing and distraction strategies Patrick had recommended. She took a long, hot bath and listened to some music before going for a walk in the park. By the time dinner came around, Mia felt a lot more settled than she had before.

She wanted to call Genevieve now but erred on the side of caution. Genevieve would still be there tomorrow, and Mia didn't want to rush things and end up messing them up. She'd messed up enough already.

So, she waited until the next morning before making her move. Mia slept without nightmares, as she usually did nowadays. She woke up early, but waited until lunch, not wanting to disturb Genevieve's routine.

Finally, at twelve-thirty, Mia acted. She wondered if Genevieve would even answer her call. The phone rang for so long that she was starting to suspect that she would be ignored, but Genevieve eventually answered.

"Hello, Mia." She sounded extremely wary, and Mia didn't blame her for that.

"Hi, Genevieve. I was wondering if we could talk."

"I'm quite busy, Mia, but if it's important, I can spare a few minutes."

Well, this wasn't off to a hopeful start, but Mia pushed on. "I was hoping we could talk in person."

"I don't think that's a good idea. What was it you needed, Mia?"

Well, she guessed they were just going to do this over the phone, then. "I've been in therapy for a while now—ever since we split up. It's been tough, but I've persevered, and I really think I'm getting a handle on my issues. I'm not completely cured, but I finally feel like I'm in a stable place. I met with my mom and explained to her exactly why I'm not going to re-establish a relationship with her. I don't think she'll contact me again—if she does, any further contact will be between her and my lawyer."

Genevieve's voice lost some of its frostiness. "That's great, Mia. I'm proud of you."

"I want you back."

Silence. Mia quickly continued before Genevieve could decide to hang up.

"I wasn't ready before, but I am, now. I love you, Genevieve, and I want to be with you. I know I've made mistakes, but I'm ready to earn back your trust, no matter how long it takes."

Genevieve sighed. "Thank you for your honesty, Mia, but I don't think that's a good idea."

This was exactly why Mia had wanted to meet in person. Over the phone, she couldn't read Genevieve's body language or facial expressions, and she needed every advantage she could get in this situation.

"Are you saying you don't love me too?"

There was a long pause. "That wasn't what I said. That's not the point, though. We can't be together, Mia."

"May I ask why not?"

"You may be committed now, but what happens when your past gets in the way again? I don't want to do things halfway, Mia."

"Neither do I. I may not have been invested enough before, but I am now, and I'm willing to prove it. Come on a date with me? Let's take things slow. If you don't like what you see—if I give you even the smallest indication that I'm not one hundred percent committed to making this work long term—you can always still leave."

There was another long pause. Mia waited on tenterhooks, hoping with all of her being that Genevieve would take her.

"No."

Mia felt like her insides shriveled at the sound of that tiny, awful word.

"I'm sorry, Mia, but I have to go. I don't think it's a good idea for us to be in contact anymore."

The line clicked dead.

Mia let her hand holding the phone drop to her side. She wasn't going to cry, because this wasn't defeat—not yet.

She had hurt Genevieve in the past. She completely understood why Genevieve may be hesitant to trust her. Mia wasn't going to let the love of her life go without a fight, though. If, once Genevieve knew how serious Mia was, she still didn't want a relationship, Mia would respect that.

First, though, she had to make Genevieve see how truly loved and wanted she was.

Mia had a plan.

11

GENEVIEVE

Genevieve was looking at her phone, again. She knew she was being stupid. She had made herself clear to Mia, and Mia was simply respecting her boundaries.

Still, Mia couldn't have been as committed as she said, if she had given up so easily, and that made it all that much harder not to wallow in her own misery and disappointment.

Genevieve knew that she was doing the right thing. It had been five weeks with no word from Mia. She was glad she hadn't said yes, given that Mia had clearly moved on from her so quickly that Genevieve was beginning to doubt Mia's assertion of love.

Maybe if she kept telling herself that enough times, she would start to believe it.

"Genevieve?"

"Yes, Penelope, come in."

Penelope had taken to checking on Genevieve. She always had a valid work excuse for it, but those excuses were things that she could easily have taken care of on her own. Genevieve didn't mind it, really. It was nice to know that people cared.

Before Mia, this would have simply annoyed her, but while she was committed to keeping herself away from personal relationships, she still appreciated Penelope's concern.

Mia had changed Genevieve permanently, and Genevieve feared she would never recover.

And she was back to moping. Genevieve forced herself to smile and look up at Penelope. "How can I help you?"

"You need to come down to the gallery with me."

"What's wrong? Has there been an accident?"

The gallery where they employed their artists had its own manager. It must be something pretty serious if they needed Genevieve down there in person.

"No, everything is fine, but you do need to go there."

"Why?" Genevieve wasn't particularly keen on going down there if there wasn't an emergency. She might run into Mia, and she definitely didn't want that. It was sure to hurt, and she was quite happy to avoid that hurt forever if she could manage it.

"You'll see. Please, just trust me?"

"Penelope, I'm busy. I don't really have time for nonsense."

"This isn't nonsense. Come on, Genevieve, it'll take less than ten minutes."

"Fine," Genevieve sighed, getting up. She and Penelope walked side by side to the gallery. Penelope was usually a complete chatterbox, but now, she was uncharacteristically silent.

Genevieve suspected a trap of some kind, but before she could think better of going along with this, they were walking into the gallery.

Genevieve stopped short in the doorway. She had never seen so many images of herself in one place before.

The entire gallery was filled with paintings, large and small, of her and Mia.

Genevieve felt tears threaten as she was

confronted with a dozen happy memories. She found herself gliding forward, running a hand over some of the paintings, remembering the dates, laughs, and little moments she and Mia had had together.

There could be only one person behind this.

Genevieve didn't have to look far before she found Mia, standing right next to one of the largest paintings—a scene of the two of them lying together in a field of sunflowers, which Genevieve recognized from one of their earlier dates.

Genevieve knew that she should say something, but she was at a loss for words.

Any words she might have said fled the scene when Mia slowly got down onto one knee, her eyes never leaving Genevieve's. Mia took a small box out of her pocket.

She opened it, revealing a sparkling diamond ring.

Genevieve's eyes flicked from the ring to Mia's face and back again, her heart pounding in her throat.

"Genevieve, there are so many things I want to say to you. So many apologies and promises, but those can come later. For now, I have only two things to say. I love you, Genevieve, and I want to be your wife. Will you marry me?"

Genevieve was barely aware of their frozen audience as she walked closer to Mia, feeling as if she was in some kind of dream. She should probably have thoughts spinning around in her head. She should be weighing the pros and cons, assessing the risks and rewards. It was what she was trained to do.

Genevieve did none of that. For perhaps the first time in her life, she made a decision purely on what she felt in her heart, logic and reason be damned.

"Yes."

There were gasps all around as Mia slid the ring onto Genevieve's finger, her face alight with fierce passion.

"You'll never regret it, I promise you that, Genevieve."

"I know. I love you, Mia." Genevieve had been a fool to believe that Mia wouldn't fight for her. Clearly, she had a lot to learn about her fiancé.

"I love you too." Mia let out a shaky laugh. "I didn't think you'd say yes."

"Neither did I. I'm glad, though."

"Me too."

Genevieve stared around at the paintings. "I can't believe you did all of these. They're spectacular."

"I've been painting pretty much nonstop for the last five weeks. Good thing, too—I thought my inspiration had dried up. I was beginning to think I may never be able to paint again... but you breathed life into my work. The memories I have with you are some of the best moments of my life, and I can't wait to make more."

"Me too, Mia." Genevieve reached for Mia, and Mia reached for her in turn. They stepped easily into each other's arms and kissed.

Around them, everyone broke out into applause.

Genevieve barely noticed.

EPILOGUE

"I don't want to take it off," Mia whined.

Genevieve raised an eyebrow. "So you'd prefer to spend the rest of our honeymoon searching for it in the snow?"

Mia considered this for a moment. "Maybe you have a point," she conceded, taking her shiny new wedding ring off her finger and tucking it safely into the hotel drawer.

Genevieve kissed her and put her own wedding ring next to Mia's. "Now, are you ready?"

"Yeah—let's do this!"

It hadn't taken long to agree on a honeymoon location. Both Mia and Genevieve had always wanted to try skiing, so Switzerland had been a natural choice.

They were booked for a skiing lesson in less than half an hour. Mia hated to see Genevieve's beautiful body covered up in bulky layers of clothes, but she didn't want her wife getting cold, so she didn't complain.

They held hands as they walked the short distance to the beginner's area, where their instructor was waiting for them.

"Genevieve? Mia? I'm Ivette—it's nice to meet you."

"Nice to meet you too." Genevieve shook Ivette's hand, and Mia did the same.

"Where do we start?" Mia was eager to go flying down the slopes, but it seemed that there was more to skiing than people on TV made it appear.

"Well, first let's get you onto your skis."

Sounded easy enough, right?

Wrong.

Mia giggled hysterically as Genevieve toppled over trying to click her second boot into place on the ski, bumping into Mia and sending them both sprawling in the snow.

"It's okay. It takes some getting used to." Ivette

held out a hand to help each of them up. Mia was still giggling under her breath, and looking at Genevieve only made it worse, so she fixed her eyes on Ivette.

"Now, you're going to use these to guide you." She handed Mia and Genevieve two long poles. "Put them in the snow and use them to steer, like this."

She demonstrated while standing still. Mia and Genevieve tried to do the same thing.

Genevieve fell over, this time taking Ivette as well as Mia down with her. Ivette was up on her feet quickly, but Mia lay draped over Genevieve's chest, shaking with laughter. "You suck at this, you know."

"Some wife you are," Genevieve grumbled, but she was laughing almost as much as Mia.

Ivette surveyed them with increasingly strained patience. "Up you get, ladies. We'll be going down this slope."

Mia looked at the slope. *Slope* was generous. It was more of a mildly angled road. "What about that one?" She pointed to one of the neighboring slopes—the real ones—that stretched so high it was hard to see the top.

Ivette raised an eyebrow. "You want your wife going down that as her first try?"

Mia glanced at Genevieve, who was still covered in snow from her first two falls. "I guess not."

Genevieve gave her a sour look, but the corners of her mouth were twitching.

"Okay, now just follow me and do exactly what I do. Don't try anything fancy."

They pushed themselves onto the slope and angled their bodies like Ivette's.

Mia didn't know how it happened. One moment, she was wobbling along down the slope, and the next, she was being dumped onto her butt.

She blinked snow out of her eyes to find Genevieve sprawled over her lap, looking just as confused as Mia felt.

"What happened?"

"Don't ask me! You're the one who fell into me."

"I did not fall into you! You got in the way and I tripped over you!"

"I didn't! You—"

Genevieve shut Mia up by kissing her. Behind them, she heard Ivette sigh.

This learning to ski thing could take some time, it seemed.

They returned to the hotel about an hour later, red in the face and covered in quickly melting snow.

"I think we're going in her book of worst clients ever. Or at least, you are."

Genevieve rolled her eyes. "You're never going to let this go, are you?"

"Nope. This is the first thing I've ever found that you suck at. We should totally come again—it'll be good for you."

"Next time I want to find something you're not good at."

"That's easy. Just put me in an office and watch my spirit wilt."

"On second thought, I prefer you here, like this." Genevieve trailed a hand down Mia's face. Mia was starting to get cold now, the rush of activity fading and making her notice things like the cool squishy feeling of her shoes against her frigid feet.

"I could use a shower. How about you?"

"I could be convinced to join you."

"I'm in a convincing mood." Mia leaned in and whispered in Genevieve's ear. "How about we try that suction dildo against the shower wall. I'd love to fuck myself on it while licking your clit until you come."

"Oh, fuck yes."

"That wasn't very hard."

"Let's just say I'm in a convincible mood. I'm quite partial to the color of your face when you've been out in the snow."

Mia took Genevieve's hand and walked backward to the shower, pulling Genevieve with her and grabbing the suction cup dildo out of the drawer on the way. They had been here for four days now, and she knew the layout. The honeymoon suite had a huge shower, which she and Genevieve had made use of multiple times now.

Genevieve turned on the hot water while Mia stripped off her soaked clothes. She paused before getting in, watching Genevieve wrestle herself out of her wet pants. Mia could have offered to help, but she was enjoying the way Genevieve's ass wiggled too much to want to change the view right now.

By the time Mia stepped into the water, it was delightfully steamy. She fiddled to get the temperature just right while Genevieve took off the last of her clothes.

Mia dipped the dildo under the water briefly and leaned down to press it against the shower wall. She tested it briefly and found that it seemed to stay on. She was super excited to try this.

Genevieve joined her, pulling Mia to her feet.

"But the dildo," Mia pouted. She was already looking forward to having it inside her at the same time as experiencing the delightful feeling of Genevieve's clit under her tongue.

"I want to kiss you first."

Mia couldn't find a single thing to object to about that sentiment, so she let Genevieve pull her close. They kissed slowly at first, exploring each other's mouths. Genevieve tasted like snow and steam and the chocolates they had shared on the way back.

Mia moaned and tilted her back, giving Genevieve access to deepen the kiss, which she did without hesitation.

Genevieve slotted one leg between Mia's, and Mia eagerly pressed herself down onto the leg, positioning herself so that it gave her some delicious pressure over her clit.

Mia reached for Genevieve's breasts, thumbing her nipples until they became hard under her touch. She pulled one nipple into her mouth while still riding Genevieve's thigh.

Genevieve put both hands on the back of Mia's

head, guiding her to the other nipple. Mia lavished it with equal attention, licking and sucking, moaning at the wildly erotic feeling of her wife's tender flesh against her tongue.

"Did you say something about the dildo?"

Mia had forgotten, but she certainly remembered now.

"Yeah." She got onto her hands and knees, positioning herself against the dildo. "A little help?"

Genevieve chuckled and leaned down, slowly guiding the dildo into Mia's pussy. Then she went to her knees on the shower floor, spreading her legs wide.

"Get me off."

Oh fuck, Mia loved it when Genevieve used that commanding tone, the one that allowed no argument—not that Mia wanted to argue.

It was tricky, as she was using her hands to brace herself, but she used her tongue to lick Genevieve open and start laving over her clit. Genevieve whimpered and thrust her hips forward. Mia licked harder and started rocking her hips against the dildo.

It was bigger than what they usually used, and

it stretched Mia to her limits, giving her a delicious feeling of fullness.

It took a few minutes to work up a good rhythm, with her moving back and forth and Genevieve's hips chasing her tongue as it went in and out of reach.

Once they got it right, it was more than worth it. Mia swiped her tongue down momentarily to taste Genevieve before coming back up to her clit. They were both panting as they moved, the hot shower water streaming over them as they breathed in the steam.

Genevieve suddenly stiffened, crying out as she came. Mia redoubled her licking, making sure to get the most out of the orgasm. Genevieve came for a long time, longer than Mia ever remembered her doing so.

She finally collapsed backward, her back hitting the shower wall with a wet smacking sound.

"Ow!"

"Are you okay?" Mia started to scramble toward her, but Genevieve put a hand on Mia's shoulder, holding her in place with the dildo still inside her. Mia stilled, her eyes roving over Genevieve's body. She didn't seem hurt, but Mia needed to be sure.

"I'm fine. I just got a surprise, that's all. Go on. I want to see you fuck yourself into an orgasm."

Mia didn't need to be told twice. She went at it on the dildo with wild abandon. She didn't often come without pressure on her clit, but she had done it before—with Genevieve, anything was possible. The wet sound of the dildo moving in and out of her pussy could barely be heard above the shower water and Mia's harsh panting.

Mia felt herself approaching release, but she couldn't quite get there. Her knees were protesting to being on the hard shower floor, but there was no way she was stopping now.

"Genevieve," Mia gasped.

Genevieve didn't need her to vocalize further. She knew what Mia needed—something to push her over the edge.

She reached down to where Mia's breasts were swinging with the motions of her body and took Mia's nipples between finger and thumb, squeezing and pulling lightly on them.

That was all Mia had needed. She slammed herself onto the dildo as her orgasm overtook her. Her thighs and shoulders strained as she kept pushing back and forth for several delicious thrusts before finally slowing.

Mia pulled off the dildo, landing inelegantly in Genevieve's lap and getting a mouthful of shower water. Genevieve chuckled as Mia spluttered, sitting up so that she didn't choke. "Now you know how I felt landing face down in the snow for the dozenth time."

"That'll be a story for the ages. I wish we'd gotten it on camera. Maybe tomorrow I can—"

"Absolutely not. I will be throwing your phone off a snowbank if I even suspect you of filming my humiliation."

Mia held her hands up in surrender. "Fine, fine. But that won't protect you. I'll remember every minute of it and remind you about it until we're old and gray."

"You—"

They both broke off at the sound of a phone ringing. Mia was the first to bolt out of the shower, with Genevieve hot on her heels. They had both set special ringtones for this particular number.

It was Genevieve's phone that was ringing. Mia tossed Genevieve a towel to dry her hands and hurried back to the bathroom to turn off the shower while Genevieve answered.

"Hello?"

Mia threw herself down onto the sofa next to

Genevieve. Both of them were still dripping wet and naked, but neither cared right now.

"Yes, this is Genevieve. I see—that's excellent. We'll be back on the fifteenth, so any date after that would work for us. No, we both work, but we can rearrange our schedules for this. Okay. Excellent, I will await your email, then. Thank you."

Mia was practically exploding with excitement as Genevieve hung up the phone.

"Our application was accepted?"

"It was!" Genevieve flung her arms around Mia, squeezing her so tightly it took her breath away.

"I can't believe it... you're going to be a great mother, you know."

"I suspect you'll be better than I am. Adoption is always tricky, and we're specifically adopting from a home that has kids with trauma. You have so much more experience in that area than I do."

"Personal experience, sure, but you have more experience in caring for someone with trauma, which will probably be more valuable in the end."

"Well then, I suppose our child will be lucky to have both of us."

"I'm a bit nervous about the appointment," Mia admitted. "There will be a lot of children there, and we're only looking to adopt one, or two at most if they're siblings. How would we even go about choosing? It feels wrong, like you're picking pets from a shelter. This is so much more than that."

"Well, they'll likely give us some files to look through. They've done a thorough look into our lives, so they will probably know which kids might be a good match for us. We're unlikely to just be dumped among then and asked to choose. I'll confirm details with them when I get the email, but from what she said, it sounded like we'd meet a couple of children, then choose one or two to foster. If that goes well after a few months, we can proceed with the adoption process."

Mia nodded. It was difficult to be anxious when Genevieve made it sound so simple and easy.

Of course, raising a child, especially one with trauma, was not going to be simple or easy, but Mia couldn't be more excited for the challenge. She was going to give this child the home she had needed when she was younger but had never had.

"Let's go do something to celebrate."

Genevieve grabbed the towel and got up. "Yeah, let's do it."

Mia beamed at her. Genevieve's life, so sterile

and cold before, was now filled with spontaneity and passion. Mia, on the other hand, had the stability and care she had craved all her life.

"What are you thinking? You're suddenly looking at me with gooey eyes."

"I'm just thinking about us. This path of ours has had so many twists and turns, but they've made us stronger, you know? I certainly haven't behaved optimally in the past, but I don't regret it, because it brought us together and made us the couple we are."

"I know what you mean. I never thought I would find someone like you, Mia. I'm so proud of you, and of how far you've come."

Mia had certainly come a long way. She had wanted to be fully healed from her trauma before she took on raising a child, especially one who already had experiences that might be triggers for Mia.

She had been nervous when she had first explained her wish to Genevieve, but Genevieve had been on board from the start, taking on a lot of the organizational stuff that she thrived on but wasn't Mia's strong suit.

"Where do you want to go?"

Genevieve shrugged. "You decide."

"Let's take a stroll down the street, then. I saw a lot of potential nice-looking restaurants there when we came in."

"That sounds perfect."

Genevieve and Mia got dressed into casual but warm clothes and headed out of their hotel room.

They joined hands as they walked down the snowy avenue.

The present was bright, and the future was even brighter.

FREE BOOK

I really hope you enjoyed this story. I loved writing it.

I'd love for you to get my FREE book- Her Boss- by joining my mailing list. My mailing list is the first place to find out about my new releases and get some cool stuff for free!

Just click on the following link or type into your web browser: https:// BookHip.com/MNVVPBP

Meg has had a huge crush on her hot older boss for some time now. Could it be possible that her crush is reciprocated? https://BookHip.com/MNVVPBP

Also, if you like CEO stories, why don't you check out
Assistant to the CEO- Book 1 in the Forever Series.

**What happens when your casual sex buddy turns out
to be your new boss?**

*Find out in this super-hot Age Gap office romance with light
BDSM throughout.*

getbook.at/ATTCEO

Printed in Great Britain
by Amazon